It was like old times.

They were talking again, like when they were teenagers. But Noah wasn't the same. The lanky, nerdy teen was now a man. A father.

He glanced over at her, his blue eyes clouded. "When I found out you'd joined the ballet company and never bothered to tell me, I figured—" He stared straight ahead, his jaw flexing.

Beth longed to reach out to him. Years ago she'd shut him out of her life. And then so had his ex. All he'd wanted was to make a family with his little girl, and his dream had been shattered.

"I'm sorry, Noah. I didn't mean to cut you out of my life."

"We can't go back and change the past, Beth. But we can learn from it."

"Can we call a truce? For Chloe? After all, it's Christmas."

Finally he looked at her. "Sure. For Chloe and for Christmas."

Wasn't that what she wanted? So why did her heart still ache? Because just like old times, being friends with Noah wasn't enough.

Lorraine Beatty was raised in Columbus, Ohio, but now calls Mississippi home. She and her husband, Joe, have two sons and five grandchildren. Lorraine started writing in junior high and is a member of RWA and ACFW, and is a charter member and past president of Magnolia State Romance Writers. In her spare time she likes to work in her garden, travel and spend time with her family.

Books by Lorraine Beatty

Love Inspired

Home to Dover

Protecting the Widow's Heart
His Small-Town Family
Bachelor to the Rescue
Her Christmas Hero
The Nanny's Secret Child
A Mom for Christmas

Rekindled Romance
Restoring His Heart

A Mom
for Christmas

Lorraine Beatty

LOVE INSPIRED BOOKS

Recycling programs
for this product may
not exist in your area.

ISBN-13: 978-0-373-71991-4

A Mom for Christmas

www.Harlequin.com

Printed in U.S.A.

You shall have no other gods before Me.
—*Exodus* 20:3

To Jovetta Ealy, a woman after God's heart, and in loving memory of her sons, Marco and Willie.

Acknowledgments

To Jon Young, who shared his structural engineering expertise with me, and who, when I told him what I wanted to do to my hero, didn't blink, but proceeded to tell me how to make it happen.

To Katie Lohr, the ballerina the Lord literally placed in my car. Her knowledge and experience with ballet and with Ballet Magnificat added so much to Beth's story.

Dr. Brad Kennedy, DC, who always has the perfect solution to any injury I decide to inflict upon my characters.

I couldn't have written this book without the three of you.

Chapter One

The air in the enclosed stairwell reeked of age, and the timeworn wooden stairs creaked with each step. The glass in the old-fashioned door rattled in protest when Bethany Montgomery grasped the knob and pushed it open.

She stepped from the narrow staircase leading to her apartment above her mother's real estate office and inhaled deeply. Even here in the broad recessed entry of the downtown building, the air was tinged with the scent of degrading metal and aged wood. The tiny black-and-white octagonal tiles on the floor from over a hundred years ago completed the picture. Everything in her hometown of DoOver, aka Dover, Mississippi, was old. And at the moment she felt the same. Old, worn-out and irrelevant. And in need of a major do-over.

Unlocking the door to the right, she entered the office of Montgomery Real Estate, her mood sinking another level. She didn't want to be here. Not in Dover, not in the office and not in Mississippi. Her life was in New York, dancing with the Forsythe Ballet Company as principal ballerina for the last six years. She'd been living her lifelong dream, thé culmination of a journey started when she was five and her mother had taken her and her sister to see a production of *The Nutcracker* in New Orleans.

Now it was all gone. Ended by a torn ACL complicated by years of overuse and damage she'd paid little attention to. Her neglect had finally caught up with her. There would be no lead roles from here on, and even a spot in the corps de ballet was doubtful. Instead she was forced to come home and work for her mother. The doctors and physical therapists had all declared her days of classical ballet over.

She refused to accept that. Others had recovered from this kind of injury and gone on to perform for years. She would be like them and she wouldn't stop working until she was on stage, *en pointe*, and once more at the top of her profession.

Beth switched on the lights, booted up the computer and scanned the small office, her gaze landing on the wall of family photos. Her throat tightened as she looked at her portrait. It was her first professional photo, and she was dressed in a white tutu, *en pointe* posed *développé croisé devant,* looking like a graceful bird. Absently she rubbed her leg, remembering the pain of the last nine months and that moment when she'd landed and heard the horrible popping sound in her knee.

Her heart dropped into her stomach, leaving a cold emptiness in its place. How was she supposed to go on from here? What was she supposed to do with her life? A sob formed in her chest, but she fought it down. She'd cried and raged enough since the accident. It hadn't changed anything and only made her feel more like a failure.

"Good morning, sweetie. I'm glad to see you up and here on time."

Beth put a smile on her face before turning to face her mother as she breezed into the office. "Did I have a choice?"

Francie Montgomery patted her shoulder before taking a seat at the desk. "Of course you do. Where you work is up to you. What you do with your life from now on is in your hands. You could open up a dance studio here in Dover."

No way. She was *not* going to be one of those failed dancers who goes home and opens up a dance school for every mother who thinks her child is the next movie star. "What I want is to dance again."

Her mother exhaled a soft sigh. "Beth, sooner or later you'll have to accept that your professional career is over. Longing for something you can't have is pointless."

"It's not over. Once I'm fully recovered, I *will* dance again. Somewhere."

Her mother came and stood in front of her. "I hope and pray that's true. But your doctors and your physical therapist think differently. You have to face the facts, sweetheart. And the sooner, the better."

It was an old argument and one of the reasons Beth had moved out of her mother's house. Though well-intentioned and motivated by love, her mom's advice had quickly grown old. Being back in the family home, where the presence of her late father lingered, had added to her distress. There was only so much heartache and sadness she could endure. With her sister,

Tori, in California for an indefinite amount of time, Beth had moved in to her apartment above the real estate office to maintain her sanity.

With her mother occupying the desk, Beth moved to the front window and stared at the early morning activity along Main Street in the small town. Her mother was right. She had to face reality. But how did she begin to accept that? How did she face each day with no direction? What could possibly fill the dark, aching void left inside that ballet had always filled?

As she turned away, movement from the office across the entryway drew her attention.

Her mom had bought the entire building when she'd opened her real estate business decades ago. The ground floor consisted of two office spaces, one on either side of the entry, each with windows facing the street and each other. In the four days since she'd moved in to the apartment, she'd assumed the other office was vacant. But now a man was moving about inside. Curious, she stepped closer to the window.

He disappeared into the back room. When he reappeared, Beth strained for a closer look. Even with his back to her, it was impossible to miss how attractive he was. He had broad shoulders beneath a long-sleeved polo shirt of deep red that highlighted his muscular back as he bent and moved. Dark jeans hugged long legs. A warm trickle of appreciation oozed along her skin. Something about the dark hair curling along the nape of his neck bumped up her interest. She peered closer, hoping to catch a glimpse of his face.

"Beth, I need to show houses this morning. I don't know when I'll be back. Is there anything you need to know before I leave?"

She tore her gaze from the intriguing figure in the other office. "I don't think so. Nothing much has changed since I worked here in high school."

Her mother smiled. "True. Change comes slowly to Dover. But we're getting better. I can't wait for you to see the Christmas celebrations Gemma introduced last year."

Beth had only come home for a few days last Christmas, and had left as soon as possible. She'd been eager to get back to prepare for the London tour, and looking at the extensive decorations and events her sister-in-law had orchestrated hadn't been of interest to her.

With her mother gone, the office grew silent, allowing Beth too much time to dwell on the losses in her life. Thankfully the phone started ringing, and the next few hours passed quickly. The man next door hadn't reappeared, but she'd been unable to get him out of her thoughts.

At noon, Beth hung the out-to-lunch sign on the door, set the lock and stepped out into the entryway. She looked forward to going upstairs and hiding in her room for a while. Maintaining a happy face for the walk-in customers and a cheery tone for the call-ins inquiring about homes for sale took a toll on her emotional reserves.

She inserted her key into the lock as the door to the other office opened, and she glanced over her shoulder. Finally she would get a glimpse of the intriguing man she'd seen this morning. The smile on her face faded when she looked at him. There was something familiar about the sky blue eyes and the angle of the chin.

"Hello, Beth."

She inhaled sharply. "Noah? Noah Carlisle. Is that

you?" She took a closer look. It was him, but he was different. Very different. This wasn't the rail-thin, awkward, nerdy friend she remembered. The thick dark glasses were gone, exposing the rich blue eyes with lashes long enough to touch his brows. The planes of his face were still angled, but maturity had added a depth to his features and a sensuous fullness to his lips. Heat flooded her cheeks at the direction of her thoughts, along with a rush of delight. She reached out and gave him a hug, only to pull back when she realized he wasn't returning the gesture. In fact, he wasn't saying anything at all. There was no warmth in his blue eyes, no welcoming smile.

"I'm surprised you remember me."

"Of course I remember you." How could he say that? Her mind flooded with wonderful memories of their friendship. It had been the most important one in her life. She'd fallen in love with him, but he'd made it painfully clear he hadn't returned her feelings. Her warm recollections drained away into a dark pool of humiliation. Suddenly self-conscious, she swallowed and brushed an errant strand of hair off her cheek, attempting to collect herself. "I was thinking about you the other day."

A muscle in his jaw flexed rapidly. "Just the other day?"

What was he saying? "Yes. I mean, I've thought about you several times over the years." His eyes were hard and cold, and there was no warmth in his tone. Noah had changed in more than looks.

A sardonic grin shifted his mouth. "That often in twelve years."

Her conscience burned. She *had* thought about him,

but she'd never bothered to do anything about it. Gathering her composure, she lifted her chin. "You look good." *Good* didn't come close. The scrawny young man she remembered had grown into a dangerously attractive man.

The bony shoulders had broadened into an impressive width above a muscular chest and biceps strained at the fabric of his shirt. His clear blue eyes were more vibrant above the high cheekbones. His thick, dark chocolate hair still persisted in falling over his forehead. But it was his air of confidence that was the most striking difference. The once shy, hesitant boy now carried himself with a confident masculinity that radiated from every pore.

"You've changed."

"I grew up." He held her gaze a long moment. "I heard you were back in town."

The disinterested tone in his voice hurt. They'd been best friends. Why was he so distant and angry? True, she hadn't stayed in touch. Her career had taken all her time and attention. Surely he understood that. She refocused on his comment. "I am. For the time being."

Noah set his jaw. "Don't you think you've chased this foolish dancing dream of yours long enough?"

She clamped her teeth together and fisted her hands to keep a lid on her anger. She didn't know what his problem was, but she'd had enough. "Foolish? I'm a professional dancer with a world-renowned ballet company. I'd hardly call that a dream."

"Are you dancing now?"

The truth pierced like a scalding poker to her heart. "No. But I will be. As soon as I heal and regain my strength." Maybe if she said it often enough, it would be true.

He shook his head. "You haven't changed a bit. Still obsessed with only one thing. Being a big-time ballerina. You don't care about anything else."

"That's not true. I care about a lot of things."

Noah arched his dark eyebrows, and one corner of his mouth hiked up. "I know what you *don't* care about. Your family and your friends. How could they compete with your dreams of fame? Good seeing you again, Bethany. Have a nice life."

He pivoted and strode out onto the sidewalk, disappearing before she could form a response. Noah had always been her biggest supporter, her cheerleader. What had she done that had turned him against her? If anyone had a right to feel angry, she did. He was the one who had rejected her affections with a shrug, leaving her burning with humiliation and pain, then put as much distance as possible between them.

Up in her cozy apartment, Beth munched on a tasteless sandwich, searching her memory for some explanation for Noah's behavior. What was he doing back in Dover anyway, and why hadn't her mother told her he was here and renting space from her?

A vague memory formed of her mother mentioning something about an old friend coming back to town, but she'd tuned it out like she did most things concerning Dover.

The ugly truth forced itself into her mind. *Because keeping in touch wasn't high on your list.* Dancing had been her passion her whole life. She'd been aware that her drive had pushed most of her relationships to the side. Even her family. But to succeed, she'd had to pour all her effort and concentration into her work. And it had paid off. For the last six years, she'd been at the top of her game. *Ambiance*, the new ballet the troupe had performed in London, which she'd helped choreograph, had been the highlight of her career and put her name in the forefront of the dance world. Until one misstep had caused an injury that put her future in jeopardy. But she'd come back. She would. Somehow.

Was losing touch with Noah a big enough reason for his attitude? It didn't make sense. All she knew was that she didn't like him being angry with her. It had been a long torturous year, starting with her injury in London last winter, two surgeries and months of painful rehab in New York before coming home. She was worn down and desperately needed a friend. Noah had always been her confidant, and he'd known exactly what to say to lift her spirits.

Until today.

Noah strode away from his office and along the sidewalk, working his jaw and trying without much success to quell the anger and hurt raging in his gut. Bethany was back. He'd known that for a while. And he'd known he'd run into her sooner or later. Sooner, actually, since her mother was his landlord.

Checking Main Street for traffic, Noah jogged across to the courthouse park, making his way to Union Street and Latimer Office Supply. The chilly November wind stung, but he welcomed it. It took his mind off seeing Beth again. He had a new business to get up and running. Carlisle Structural Solutions was all he should be thinking about.

After paying for his supplies and picking up a sand-

wich at the DoOver Deli on the corner, Noah returned
to his office and settled in the back room. The first bite
of his sandwich triggered a memory—one he didn't
welcome. He'd ordered the deli's special club sandwich—Beth's favorite. He'd forgotten that. He shoved
the meal aside.

He'd forgotten a lot of things about Beth. Like how
lovely she was. When she'd turned and faced him, his
mouth had gone dry. His palms had grown sweaty, and
his heart rate tripled. He was eighteen again and in love
with his best friend. The years had faded away, along
with the pain of her desertion and her callous indifference toward those who cared about her. All he saw
was her hazel eyes that always sparkled, her kissable
mouth and the way she stirred his protective instincts
when she was close. The pink sweater with the wide
collar added a rosy tinge to her cheeks and made her
look very touchable. Her dark hair was cut in a way
that made it float around her face, and when a strand
had landed on her cheek, he'd had to stop himself from
brushing it aside.

Then she'd hugged him, and he'd slammed into a
wall of searing emotions, unable to move. She'd been
soft and warm against him. He hadn't been prepared
for that kind of response. He'd fought against the tender emotions, which had only brought out his long buried resentment. He'd spoken harshly, aware of the hurt
he'd caused her from the look in her eyes, but unable
to stop the stinging words.

Beth had severed their friendship with one quick
cut and never looked back. That's when Noah realized
that as far as she was concerned, nothing and no one
was as important to her as her life in the dance world.

Until today, he had believed he'd recovered from his broken heart and her disregard for their friendship. But like a punctured water line, all his emotions were spewing forth. In the meantime he'd have to shut off the emotional flood and keep his distance from Bethany until she left again. Easier said than done. He was always keenly attuned to her nearness, and he'd never been able to keep her from flitting through his brain like a butterfly, touching down lightly here and there, bringing memories to life again.

He glanced around the back room of his new office. He still had a lot to do to get his engineering business up and running. In the meantime he was working full-time for the city of Dover as a building inspector. Not his first choice of jobs, but it paid the bills. Thankfully, he'd be spending most of his time conducting on-site work, and there'd be no need to interact with Beth. Besides, she'd be gone soon enough, back to the only thing that ever mattered to her. Dancing. Then life would go on as usual. And he could forget Beth. Again.

Tossing his trash in the bin in the small kitchen area, Noah locked up and headed out. He had four inspections to do this afternoon. He fought the urge to glance into the real estate office to see if Beth was there, scolding himself for his weakness. He would *not* look. Stepping onto the sidewalk, he went straight to his car and climbed in, shutting down all thoughts of his old friend, fully aware of the uncomfortable truth he'd denied for years.

Bethany Montgomery had taken root in his heart, and there was no yanking her out.

* * *

Beth rubbed her eyes, trying to focus on the listings on the computer screen. After a restless night she'd wanted nothing more than to sleep in, hide under the covers and try to forget her life was in shambles. Her sister's apartment was perfect for isolating herself. Tori had a good eye for decorating, and she'd designed the space in soft muted tones of green and blue that wrapped around you like a warm hug. The balcony, which overlooked the courthouse square across the street, was shielded from curious eyes by large pots of evergreen vines that even in the dead of winter provided privacy.

But today her new job required her to be in the office bright and early. Her mother had a long list of showings, which meant Beth would be working alone most of the day. Not a pleasant prospect because it allowed her too much time to think.

She'd fretted over Noah's icy reception all night, but still found only one logical explanation. He hadn't forgiven her for not staying in touch. Noah didn't have a mean bone in his body, but he'd behaved like a man with a giant chip on his shoulder. A man who had been deeply hurt. But not by her. He'd never loved her. The realization still had the power to bring a sharp prick to her heart. She planned on talking to him again once he calmed down. If he did. She had enough to worry about as it was.

Shutting down thoughts of her old friend, she concentrated on sorting through the new additions on the Multiple Listing Service and the few phone messages left by locals who were putting their homes on the market. Thankfully the day passed quickly. It was early afternoon when the office door swooshed open. She looked up, expecting house hunters. Instead, a young girl walked in and slowly made her way toward the reception desk, her gaze scanning the walls as she went.

She was a cute child with golden brown hair in a page-boy style that framed her oval face and brought out her big blue eyes. Beth guessed her to be about the same age as her niece, Abby. She leaned her forearms on the desk. "Are you looking to buy a home, or are you more interested in renting?"

The little girl giggled. "I'm not looking for a house. I'm only nine. I'm here to look at the pictures." She pointed to the wall of family portraits and photographs her mother proudly displayed.

"I see. Shouldn't you be in school?"

"Dentist appointment." The girl stepped to the desk and extended her hand. "I'm Chloe. I come in here a lot to look at the pictures when Miss Francie is here. Oh." Her eyes grew wide, and her mouth fell open. "You're her. I mean you're you, I mean—" She swallowed and pointed to the ballet portrait. "That's you, isn't it?"

Beth smiled and nodded. "Yes, it is."

Chloe's eyes grew soft and dreamy, and she clasped her hands together over her heart. "You're beautiful. Like a white butterfly floating in the air."

Her throat contracted. Never had she received such a sweet and sincere compliment. "Thank you, Chloe. That means a lot to me."

"I want to be a ballerina. I want to drift like a feather and wear beautiful costumes." She spread her arms and twirled around the office.

Beth couldn't help but smile. The child was adorable. "Well, you can if you work hard. It takes a lot of training and dedication. Do you take dance lessons now?"

Chloe stopped. Her arms dropped to her sides, and her expression sagged nearly to the floor. "No. I can't."

She spoke the words with such drama that Beth had to swallow the chuckle that rose in her throat. "Why not?"

Chloe plopped her elbows on the desk, resting her chin in her hands. "Because my dad thinks it's a waste of time, and he doesn't want me to get caught up in silly dreams."

Beth frowned and pressed her lips together. What kind of parent would tell a child such a ridiculous thing? "Dancing isn't silly or a waste of time. It is a beautiful way to express emotion. It builds muscle and teaches discipline."

"Daddy thinks it's better if I play sports. He says they build character and teach a whole bunch of life lessons and stuff."

Typical male. She could hear her brothers making the same argument. "What does your mother say?"

"Oh, she's not here. She and Daddy got divorced a long time ago. She lives in Hollywood and has her own TV show. It's called *Brunch with Yvonne St. James.*" Chloe's eyes brightened, and she came around to stand beside Beth. "She's going to send me a plane ticket so I can spend Thanksgiving with her, and she's going to put me on her show, and I'll get to meet lots of famous people. I hope I can meet Dustin Baker. I love his music, and he's so dreamy."

Beth had no idea who that was, but obviously he made Chloe's little heart beat faster. "Are you going alone to see your mom?"

"Yes, ma'am. I can't wait."

Beth hadn't been addressed as *ma'am* in a long time, and hearing it now set her back. It was common, even expected, here in the South, but having it directed at her made her feel older than her thirty years.

"I've seen lots of pictures of you."

"You have?"

Chloe nodded. "Your mama talks about you a lot." She pointed to the picture wall again. "I know your whole family. Those are your big brothers, Linc and Gil, and that's their new wives, Gemma and Julie. Oh, and that's Evan and Abby." She walked toward the wall. "That's Seth and Tori, but they aren't here now 'cause Seth is in school to be a policeman and Tori is in California. I wonder if she knows my mom?"

"California is a pretty big place."

Chloe shrugged. "I wish I had a big family. It's just me and my dad. Oh, and my gram."

"I've noticed you're limping. Did you hurt yourself?"

She glanced down at her knee and shrugged. "I have Alls Goods Ladder."

"She means Osgood-Schlatter."

Beth's pulse throbbed at the sound of Noah's rich voice. She hadn't heard him come in, nor had she expected to see him again so soon. He barely gave her a glance now.

"Chloe, what are you doing here? I told you to stay in my office."

"Hi, Daddy. I wanted to see the pictures, and I got to meet the ballerina. I mean Miss Beth. Isn't she beautiful?"

An awkward silence fell over the room like a suffocating blanket. Beth kept her gaze averted as Noah placed his hands on his daughter's shoulders in a protective gesture. Noah was a father? She hadn't considered that. She'd heard he'd gotten married not long after he'd moved to California, which had added another spear to her punctured heart. Noah had never thought of her as anything other than a friend. His buddy.

She swallowed and grasped for control. "Osgood's. That's a knee problem, isn't it?"

He nodded. "She injured her knee playing soccer and then had a growth spurt, which complicated things." He squeezed Chloe's shoulder. "She's supposed to do her physical therapy exercises every day, but it's like pulling teeth."

"I hate them. They hurt and they're boring."

Beth could sympathize. "I know exactly how you feel. I had surgery on my knee, and I have to do PT exercises every day, too. It's not fun, but if you're going to get stronger and play soccer, you have to do them faithfully."

Chloe screwed up her mouth and crossed her arms over her chest. "Great. I was hoping you'd be on my side."

Beth chuckled softly. "The exercises don't have to be boring. You can listen to music—that usually helps."

"Is that what you do?"

She nodded. "I put on my favorite ballet warm-up music and pretend I'm dancing. You know dancing can help strengthen the other muscles in your legs and knees and speed your recovery."

"Really? Dad, can Miss Beth teach me to dance? I'll do my exercises if I can dance. Please?"

The deep scowl on Noah's face made it clear he was

unhappy with her suggestion. "Chloe, go on back to my office and collect your things. We're going home."

"Okay. 'Bye Miss Beth."

The minute Chloe was gone, Noah approached her, his eyes narrowed and dark. "I'd appreciate it if you wouldn't encourage her to come over here."

"Why? Apparently she visits my mother frequently."

"That's different. Your mother will always be here. You won't. You said yourself you'll be leaving as soon as you're fully recovered."

She had told him that even though she knew it wasn't true. "And what does that have to do with Chloe visiting me?"

"I don't want you filling her head full of ideas about your dancing career."

Now she understood, sort of. "Is that why you don't want her to take dancing lessons? Because of me?"

"Don't flatter yourself. I want her to grow up with a practical, realistic view of the world, and I don't want her sidetracked by pointless dreams of being a dancer or an actress or any of those careers that lead to disappointment."

"Little girls need to dream, Noah. You had a few dreams, as I recall."

He nodded in acknowledgment, but his gaze still held condemnation. "But I grew up and realized that dreams don't come true."

"You're wrong. Dreams are what gives us hope and joy."

"Hope and joy?" He shook his head. "Disappointment and heartbreak. Look where your dream has left you. I want better for Chloe."

The hurt in his light blue eyes and the pain that

pulled at the corner of his mouth stabbed like an ice pick to her heart. What had happened to turn the sweet, understanding boy she'd loved into an angry, closed-off man?

He held up his hands as if to ward off further discussion. "Just stop telling her dancing can help with her recovery."

"It can. In fact, ballet is being used as therapy for people with Parkinson's and a variety of other medical conditions. At the very least, it'll encourage her to do her exercises. I've been through countless physical therapy sessions over the years, and the only way to get through much of it is to make it fun. What harm can it do?"

"Harm? Next she'll want to be a dancer like you, and look where that leads."

"Where does it lead, Noah? I had a wonderful career. I achieved everything I set out to accomplish. I fulfilled my dream."

"But what did it cost you along the way? What did you give up to capture that dream, Beth? Was it really worth it?" He yanked open the door and left.

Beth clenched her teeth. She wanted to shout at him that yes, it had been worth it, but the words wouldn't come. Why? She'd always been so sure of her direction, her purpose. She'd been blessed with a gift, and she'd used it to the fullest. Until the injury had derailed her future. But she'd make a comeback. She was still working out in her old studio at her mom's house each morning. That's what she wanted, wasn't it? To dance even if it wasn't as the lead?

A small voice whispered in her ear. *Is* that what she wanted? Or was it what she was doing because there was nothing else? The last two years had taken a toll not only on her body, but also on her passion. She was still trying to sort out the shifts in her emotions from the accident. Now she was trying to swim through gelatin and figure out who she was and where she wanted to go.

Beth watched Noah walk away. Twelve years ago she'd handed him her heart, the bravest thing she'd ever done, and he'd tossed it aside. He'd gone on with his life, gotten married and had a child. He hadn't bothered to contact her, so why was she the bad guy?

She looked across the entryway to Noah's office as he and Chloe walked out. Chloe waved over her shoulder, a mischievous smile on her face. Dad may have laid down the law, but she had a feeling Chloe would find a way to come and visit her again. And she would make sure to invite her, despite what Noah had said.

Chapter Two

Noah parked the car behind the historic mansion and shut off the engine. The twelve-room Victorian home was one of the oldest in Dover. His great-great-grandparents had founded Dover, then known as Junction City, in the mid-1800s. After the great fire that destroyed many of the wooden structures, the town was rebuilt and renamed Do Over, which had evolved into Dover. The town's most prominent citizens built their homes to the east of town, along Peace Street. Only half of the dozen original opulent dwellings remained. His grandmother refused to live anywhere else, despite the home being too large for her to care for and having more room than one woman needed.

Chloe darted ahead of him onto the broad back porch and into the house. Gram was one of the reasons he'd come home to Dover. He'd been fourteen when his dad's small plane had crashed, killing him and Noah's mother. He'd come here to live with Gram and Gramps. Now that Gram was alone and getting older, he'd moved in to help her out and give his daughter a chance to know her family.

Dover would hopefully provide a new beginning for him and Chloe. Dissatisfied with the hectic pace of life in San Francisco, he'd resigned from the large engineering firm he'd worked for and decided to start his own structural engineering company in Dover. His hometown would also be a more conservative place to raise Chloe, who was growing up too quickly for his liking.

His grandmother, Evelyn Carlisle, was in the kitchen listening to Chloe recount her day. He noticed Gram was using her cane today—a sign her arthritis was flaring up again.

"I wish I could be like her." Chloe sighed loudly, a dreamy look on her face.

"Like who?"

"Miss Beth."

Noah shrugged out of his coat and draped it over the back of the chair. "No. You don't." He turned and saw a scowl on his gram's face. He probably shouldn't have said that, but he didn't want his daughter's head filled with notions of chasing fame.

"Yes, I do. She's beautiful. I wish I could see her dance. I've only seen pictures."

"I understand she is quite amazing. A very successful ballerina." Gram raised her eyebrows. "She and your father were close friends in high school."

Chloe grabbed his arm. "Really? Are you serious? You knew her? Did you see her dance? Was she gorgeous? Did she float like a dandelion puff?" Chloe spread her arms and twirled around the kitchen, bumping into the island.

"I never saw her dance." Strange how he'd never realized that until now. He'd seen her in her studio warming up, but he'd never actually attended a performance. They'd been best friends, had shared everything, but at eighteen the thought of going to a ballet hadn't been an option, even for a nerd like he'd been.

Chloe's eyes widened. "I'm sure I could find videos of her on the internet. Can I look? Please?"

Refusal was on the tip of his tongue, but the pointed look from his gram told him to give in. She wasn't above pointing out his parenting shortcomings. He really needed his own place, but he couldn't leave her alone in this big house. "You can use my tablet, but sit here at the kitchen table to search."

Chloe scooped up the device and started tapping the screen.

Gram put the finishing touches on the sandwiches she was preparing and handed him the plate. He plucked a stem of grapes from the fruit bowl and grabbed a couple of cookies from the jar before taking a seat at the island.

"I wondered how long it would take you to run into Beth again. She's been home a while now."

"How do you know that?"

"Francie told me."

He'd forgotten that his gram and Beth's mom were good friends. But then, he'd forgotten a lot about this place. He'd only been back in town a couple of months himself. "I ran into her yesterday."

Gram set her own plate of food on the counter. "Hmm. That explains why you came home hissing like a snared alligator."

"I did not."

Gram shrugged. "How does she look? Has she changed much?"

"She's too thin. But I guess she has to be. Her hair is shorter." Softer looking, and it framed her face in long curvy strands that caressed her cheeks and made him want to brush them aside and feel the silky softness. "But otherwise she hasn't changed." She still had the sweet, childlike smile that made him want to hug her. Her hazel eyes, with their sooty lashes, were still as beguiling as ever, though they held a darker shade to them now. Maturity? Or sadness?

"Chloe seems taken with her."

"Not for long. Beth told me herself that as soon as she's recovered she's going back to the ballet."

Gram studied him a long moment. "I don't think that's going to happen. Francie told me that her injury was career-ending. She'll never dance professionally as a ballerina again. She's facing an uncertain future."

The bite of sandwich stuck in Noah's throat. No. Gram had to be wrong. "Are you sure? She looked fine to me." More than fine. He shut down that thought.

"That fall she took destroyed her knee, and then there were complications."

"What fall?"

"Noah, don't you know what happened?"

He didn't have a clue. He'd made it a point not to keep track of her successes. "I knew she'd been injured, but that's all."

"Oh, it was a terrible thing. She was doing one of those big leaps and landed wrong and tore her ACL. Her mother thinks Beth is in denial over her situation. It's very sad. That child was born to dance."

That was one thing Noah could not deny. "Yes. She was." The thought of Beth never dancing again left an unfamiliar chill in his chest. As much as he resented her passion for the dance, and the way she'd shut out everyone, he knew how much it meant to her. It had shaped her entire life. How would she cope without it? What was she going to do now?

"Daddy, I found some videos. Can I watch them?"

Reluctantly, he nodded. Chloe sat beside him, and he couldn't resist glancing at the tablet as she scrolled through the selection of clips featuring Bethany Montgomery. There were dozens. "Pick three. That's all."

Chloe clicked on the one labeled Aurora's Act 3 Variation in *The Sleeping Beauty*. He had no idea what that meant, but he couldn't force himself to look away. Beth appeared in a short tutu jutting out from her tiny waist. The puffy sleeves of her costume highlighted the graceful curves of her neck and shoulders. She rose on her toes, her arms floating gracefully as she began to dance with quick, precise steps. Part of him wanted to watch. To see her passion in action. But then reality shoved its way into his thoughts. There was only room for one love in her life, and it hadn't been him. That's what he had to remember.

Pushing back from the table, he carried his plate to the sink, then headed for the room off the parlor that had once been his grandfather's office. Now it was his. He had a four-inch binder of Mississippi building codes to study. He focused on the numbers in front of him, but he couldn't fully shake the vision of Beth on the screen, moving as if gravity had no claim on her. Even in the few moments he'd watched, her joy as she performed was impossible to miss. The thought of his Beth never dancing again was a cruel twist of fate he'd never have wanted for her.

His Beth. Ha. She'd never been his, even if that's

how he'd always thought of her. He'd fallen for Beth from the first moment he'd started tutoring her in math their senior year. She'd missed several weeks of school due to illness, and when the teacher had approached him about helping her catch up, he'd jumped at the chance. They'd quickly become friends. Neither of them had fit in well at school, and their friendship had filled a void for both of them.

He'd been sullen and withdrawn, burying himself in school and video games. Beth had been the shy, pretty girl, a self-proclaimed dance geek. Her friendship had drawn him out of his lingering anger and grief over losing his parents, and had brought a new life and light to his existence. He'd never confessed his true feelings, fearing it would destroy their relationship. Deep down he'd believed a gangly, self-conscious guy like him had little chance with an elegant, talented girl like Beth.

But something had changed between them those last months before graduation. Beth had auditioned for the Forsythe Company but hadn't made the cut. She was devastated, and he'd done all he could to comfort and encourage her. The incident had drawn them closer together, and Noah had seen a new sparkle in her hazel eyes and a more intimate curve to her lips when she smiled at him. They'd touched more, laughed more and shared longing looks. He'd been certain it was love.

But he'd been wrong. She'd walked out of his life without so much as a goodbye, leaving him emotionally bleeding and giving him his first lesson in believing in dreams.

It was only later that he learned a position had opened up with the ballet suddenly, and Beth had gone to New York to pursue her dancing dream. That's when the truth had hit. Hard. In Beth's life, dance came first. Always. Friends were easily discarded, like an old pair of toe shoes. Dreams of a future with Beth were just that. Empty dreams. And dreams didn't come true. It was a lesson he would learn well over the years.

It was probably good he'd never revealed his heart. Rejecting his friendship had been painful enough. Rejecting his love would have been too humiliating to bear. For the time being, he'd stick to his plan. Avoid Beth at all costs, and when she was gone he could pick up and move forward.

But how would Beth move forward? Who would help her face the loss of the thing she loved most? An unwanted flicker of protectiveness pinged along his nerves.

It wasn't his problem. She'd made her choice, and she would have to adjust to the consequences.

"Please, Daddy, let Miss Beth teach me how to dance. I promise I'll do my exercises every day."

Noah placed the salt and pepper shakers in the cupboard after supper that night. Chloe had talked of nothing else all through the meal. "Just because Miss Beth thinks dancing is a good idea doesn't mean it is. It could make your injury worse."

Silverware clanged as Gram placed it in the dishwasher. "I think it's a wonderful idea. She needs something to encourage her to do those exercises."

Noah shut the cabinet door with more force than necessary. "Chloe is fine. She just needs to do what she's supposed to."

Gram exhaled a puff of air as she glared over her glasses. "I'm supposed to exercise for my arthritis, too, but it's uncomfortable so I don't do it. I know it'll help eventually, but getting to the 'eventually' part takes too long. Why don't you talk to Pete Jones, her physical therapist, and see what he says? Or better yet, have Pete consult with Beth about the pros and cons of letting her dance."

"Out of the question."

"Honestly." Gram faced him, a deep scowl on her face. "Would you feel the same if it was anyone other than Beth? I would have thought you'd have gotten over her long ago."

"There was nothing to get over. We were friends. It ended. I simply don't want Chloe getting silly dreams in her head. I want her to have a secure future and a job that will provide a good living. Not something like dancing that could end suddenly or never take off at all."

Gram placed the decorative candle back in the center of the breakfast room table. "Like moving to Hollywood and having your own talk show."

Noah set the tea pitcher in the fridge and shut the door. "I didn't say that."

"You didn't have to." Gram untied her apron and hung it on a peg at the end of the counter. "Have you heard from Yvonne?"

Noah groaned softly. Another sore subject. His ex-wife and her utter disregard for their child. "Not since she texted Chloe about sending her a plane ticket to come out to Los Angeles for Thanksgiving."

"Do you think she'll follow through?"

"No. And I'll have to tell my daughter yet again that her mother is too busy with her career to find time to spend with her."

"Maybe having time with Beth and learning to dance would help soften the blow."

Noah ground his teeth. "Until Beth packs up and heads back to New York without warning. Chloe doesn't need another woman in her life pushing her aside when something more exciting comes along."

"Are you so sure that'll happen? Her mother says her ballet career is over."

Noah shook his head. "You don't know Beth the way I do. If she makes up her mind to dance again, then she will. It's the only thing she really cares about."

"That's understandable. She devoted her life to being a ballerina, and I know how competitive the dance world is. She had to give it one hundred percent of her time and focus to succeed."

"No. She had to give up everything and every*one* to succeed." He glanced at his gram, intending to drive home his point, but she was looking back at him with a knowing expression and a glint in her blue eyes as if she'd discovered something delightful.

"You know, most friendships fade away after school. Why are you still hanging on to this one?"

"I'm not hanging on. She was a friend I thought I could count on, and she wasn't. The only thing I can depend on with Beth is that she'll leave." He ran a hand through his hair. "Her being back just reminds me that when it comes to women, my judgment is useless."

"Oh, I don't think so." She sat down. "You're a lot like your father was. He felt things deeply, but he didn't express them. He had a tender heart and it was easily wounded. He fell in love with your mother the moment they met. They worked together for two years before he even asked her out. He almost lost her to another guy because he was afraid to share his feelings."

"I don't have feelings. She killed those long ago."

"Beth did—or was that Yvonne's doing?"

Noah was not having this conversation. "Gram, I love you, but I'm a big boy. I can manage my own life." He strode from the room, but not before hearing a skeptical huff from his grandmother. She always claimed she knew him better than he knew himself. Unfortunately, she was usually right.

Bethany scrolled through the MLS for Dover and the nearby areas looking for a four-bedroom, two-bath ranch on ten acres. She'd tuned in Christmas music on the radio, and the mellow notes of "White Christmas" filled the air, but keeping her focus was a challenge. After a while the houses all began to look the same. She could never understand how her mother derived so much satisfaction from hunting down homes for sale and finding people to buy them. She printed out a couple of prospects, then stood and walked to the back room to get a fresh glass of sweet tea.

She was grateful to her mom for paying her to work at Montgomery Real Estate, but she'd have to find something else to do if she stayed in Dover. The thought gouged a channel across her stomach. She didn't want another job. She wanted to dance. It's all she'd ever wanted. But if she listened to her doctors and her physical therapist, she wouldn't be returning to the Forsythe Company. They felt certain with enough recovery time and continued PT she'd be able to dance, but classical ballet was not recommended. It would be too easy to sustain the same injury again.

Beth refused to accept their diagnosis. She'd heard of many ballerinas who had suffered an ACL reconstruction and went on to dance for several more years. She *would* dance again. She had to. What else was there for her? Eight to five in her mother's office? She wasn't qualified for much else. She'd given up her chance at a degree when she'd joined the Forsythe Company.

The office door opened as she came back into the front, and she smiled as Evelyn Carlisle walked in. "Miss Evelyn, what a nice surprise. How are you?"

She laid down the papers she was carrying and gave Beth a warm hug. "I'm not bad for an old lady with arthritis. It's nice to have our famous ballerina back with us. I know your mom is tickled pink to have you home. I love having Noah and Chloe with me again. Of course, I'm not one to sit in a rocker on the porch."

The woman's warm smile and zest for life made Beth smile. Noah's gram was always involved in something, always trying new things and always first to jump in to tackle a challenge. "What's keeping you so busy these days?"

Evelyn held up one of the papers. "This. I've reopened the Dawes Little Theater, and we're having a special Christmas performance."

Beth took the large colorful poster depicting iconic Christmas events. A sugar plum fairy, children around a tree, a winter scene and the nativity. "This looks wonderful. What made you decide to reopen the theater?"

"Your sister-in-law, Gemma. She did such a fantastic job with our celebrations last year that everyone is fired up to make this year even better. I'd been thinking about starting the little theater up again, and this seemed like the perfect opportunity. We've scheduled it for the third Saturday in December. I was hoping to put a poster in your window."

"Of course. I'll put it up right away." The thought of reviving the theater sent her heart skipping. It had been a vital part of the town for years, and she'd performed in several shows. She'd been sad to learn from her mother that Evelyn had closed it because of lack of participation.

"Most of our numbers are musical. Three familiar Christmas scenes with singing and dancing. I wanted it to be happy and joyful. We've been blessed so many people were eager to volunteer to put on the show." Evelyn adjusted her glasses. "Of course, things happen. And we're about to lose a key member of our staff. Allison Kent, our dance coordinator, just received a job offer in Biloxi she's been hoping for, and she has to start immediately."

"That's too bad." Evelyn was staring pointedly, triggering an uneasy feeling in Beth's stomach.

"I thought perhaps I could talk you into stepping into her place to help us out?"

"Me?" The idea sent a swell of excitement along her nerves. Being in a theater again, performing, the excitement, the joy. Cold reality quickly squelched the feelings. She wasn't in any shape to perform, and being in a theater now would only point out what she could no longer have. "I'm not really sure how long I'm going to be here, and I promised to help my mother." She was hedging, and the look on Evelyn's face said she knew it, too.

"Since all of our performers are amateurs, Allison kept the dances simple. They're all set, and everyone knows them by heart. All you'd have to do is keep things on track."

"That's very kind of you to ask, but…"

Evelyn patted her arm. "Just think about it. We could really use your help. Oh, and I wanted to tell you I liked your suggestion about Chloe taking dancing lessons. I think it would make doing her PT exercises easier."

"Noah told you about that?"

"He did, and I told him he was being closed-minded about the whole thing."

"What does he have against it? I really can't figure that out."

Evelyn's eyes sparkled. "Oh, well, it's a long story. He's got some funny ideas about the arts that, if you ask me, he needs to get over." She scooped up the rest of the circulars. "Well, I need to get going, or I'll never get these distributed." She stopped at the door. "Oh. If you wouldn't mind, I'd like you to take a look at the scene from *The Nutcracker* we're doing in the show. Allison had doubts about some of the steps. With your professional experience, maybe you could stop by and offer a few changes to make it better?"

It would be rude to refuse. "Of course. Just let me know."

"Thank you. Oh, and would you see that Noah gets one of these posters for his office window when he comes in?"

"Of course." Beth said goodbye, then returned to the desk and sank down in the chair. It might be fun to get involved with the production. But how would she feel being in a theater, knowing she might never dance professionally again? No. It would be safer to keep her focus on her recovery.

She was doing all she could, following her doctor's and physical therapist's advice to the letter. She was eating right, getting plenty of rest and doing her exercises faithfully. Each morning she did her exercises and a full ballet warm-up in the small studio her father had built for her when she was a child. Each day she pushed just a little harder, stretched a tiny bit farther, but always wearing her brace and careful not to overdo. She believed in her heart that if she worked hard enough and long enough, she could recapture the life she had before.

But what if the doctors were right, and she was lying to herself? That question lay like a shard of ice in her chest that never went away.

She glanced out the window and saw Noah unlocking the door to his office. Picking up the poster, she followed him inside. "Your gram left this for you to put in your window. I have one, too."

He scanned the colorful announcement with a shake of his head. "She got it into her head to start the little theater up again."

"You don't sound pleased about that."

He shrugged. "If it makes her happy…"

"She asked me to help out with the dancers. Apparently her instructor is moving away."

Noah held her gaze, his mouth in a tight line. "I suppose you jumped at the chance."

"I haven't decided yet."

"Really." He rested his hands on his hips. "What's holding you back? Too busy selling real estate? Or is little theater beneath you? Going from principal dancer to small town choreographer is quite a comedown."

"That's a horrible thing to say."

"Not if it's true."

The hurt tone in his voice made her stop and study him more closely. "Noah, what happened to you? To us? We were close friends. We always supported each other. I was going to be the famous dancer, and you were going to design architectural wonders."

Noah sat on the edge of his desk, arms crossed over his chest. "I figured out pretty quick I didn't have the imagination needed to be a successful architect. I was better suited for engineering. Numbers and equations. Things that are always solid and predictable." He stood and went around the desk. "I learned to look at the future more realistically." He faced her, his blue eyes cold. "I learned a lot that year. Like who my real friends were, and who could be depended on and who couldn't."

"We used to depend on each other."

"I thought so—until you ran off to New York and never looked back. I guess friendship didn't count as much as pursuing your career."

How could she make him understand? "I had no choice. The call came in, and I had to be in New York the next day to begin rehearsing. My mom and I were running around packing, trying to make plane reservations. It was hectic."

"Too hectic to find a second to call your *friend* and share the good news?"

His barb made a direct hit. "I meant to call you and explain."

Noah's gaze searing into hers. "When? The next day? The next week? I had to find out about you joining the ballet company in the newspaper." He worked his jaw, his eyes dark. "That's how much our friendship meant to you."

"It meant a great deal to me. But I didn't think it meant much to you."

"I waited in the gazebo until midnight for you to show up. I called you a dozen times. I finally called your house and talked to one of your brothers, but all they knew was that something had come up and you and your mom had left."

Her heart sank. They'd agreed to meet that evening at the gazebo to exchange gifts. Noah was leaving for the summer semester at Mississippi State the next morning. She hadn't shown up at the gazebo because after he'd rebuffed her affections earlier in the day, she'd wanted to avoid him. It had been easy to dismiss that night amid all the rush to leave. Is that what was behind his attitude? Her failure to show up to say goodbye?

"I'm sorry, Noah, I was so busy. You know how crushed I was when I wasn't chosen after my audition. This sudden opening with the company was the answer to my dreams."

Noah worked his jaw from side to side. "And your dream trumped a casual friendship. I get it. We all have priorities, and I learned yours that night." He stood. "Now if you'll excuse me, I have work to do."

Without a word, he walked to the back office, leaving her alone, a hundred questions swirling in her mind.

Seated at her desk again, Beth replayed the events of that last day with Noah. She couldn't tell him how heartbroken and embarrassed she'd been by his rejection. It wasn't his fault she'd read too much in to their friendship. She couldn't remain friends and pretend to be happy when he found someone else.

And he had. She'd heard through her mother that he'd abruptly transferred from Mississippi State to Stanford and married a year later. Proving once and for all his heart had never been hers. Her last thin strand of hope had died. It hadn't been a misunderstanding. He truly hadn't loved her.

With her mother out of the office, Beth tried to work, but her gaze kept wandering to Noah's office. He never appeared again. He was either really busy in the back room, or he'd slipped out the back door to avoid seeing her.

A lump formed in her throat. Noah had been more than a friend. He'd been her strong shoulder, her soft place to fall. The man she'd loved. But she'd never told him that. She'd always worried that to do so would ruin the special bond between them. When she'd finally found the courage to open her heart, he'd been embarrassed and uncomfortable. He'd made it clear that the words of love she'd had engraved on the small key chain she'd given him weren't welcome.

A sudden contradiction formed in her mind. If Noah had no feelings for her back then, why was he still so upset that she'd left town without telling him? His bristly attitude and his cutting comments didn't sound like someone who had forgotten the past. They sounded like someone who still carried the pain.

What that meant, she had no idea. In the past, if she was confused about something, she would go to Noah and discuss it with him. No subject was off limits. But now, when she was so confused, he was the last person she could turn to. The realization stung.

She had to find a way to repair their relationship because being at odds with Noah hurt more deeply than she'd thought possible.

Noah's encounter with Beth wore on his nerves like a pebble in his shoe. Thankfully, his job with the city had kept him busy all afternoon doing structural inspections, but he couldn't shake the fact that he owed her an apology. He'd been rude and hurtful. What had happened, or not happened, between them was in the past. Beth had a right to live her life. Just because seeing her again stirred up old emotional wounds wasn't her fault. He needed to recommit to his original plan. Stay away. Keep his distance. Then everything would be fine.

The tension in the kitchen was as thick as soup when he arrived home that night. Gram was at the stove, stirring the contents of a pot with vigor. Chloe was hunched up in the sunroom, her thumbs flying over her cell phone. He debated which female to approach first. Gram seemed less threatening.

He moved to the stove and looked down at the contents of the pot. "So did the sauce talk back to you, or was it Chloe?"

She huffed out a breath and straightened, peering over the rim of her glasses. "Neither. Merely a run-in with that brick wall we've been living with for the last few weeks. Apparently, the Carlisle stubborn streak didn't skip a generation."

Now he understood. "Chloe won't do her exercises."

"She says she will if Bethany teaches her to dance." Gram stopped stirring and faced him. "What can it hurt, Noah? She's nine. It's not like she's going to run off and join a ballet company at her age. This thing you have with keeping her away from anything involving the arts is just plain silly."

Noah rubbed his forehead. "I'm just trying to protect her."

"From what? Exploring new things and having fun? You can't control what your daughter dreams about, Noah. Sooner or later you have to face the fact that she's going to grow up and leave you, too. She'll make a life of her own. Denying her things she wants to do will only hasten that along, and I know you don't want that."

He knew that, but he could keep her focused on things that were more productive. Things that would instill solid values for life and a future family. He took a seat in the sunroom on the footstool across from Chloe and stretched out his palm. She sighed and handed over her phone. That was their deal. She could have a cell phone, minus internet access, and he had the right to check her call and text history. "Shouldn't you be doing your exercises?"

"They hurt."

"Don't you want to play soccer in the spring?"

"I want to dance."

"There aren't any dance schools in Dover."

"Miss Beth could show me. She's famous. She knows all about dancing."

Every word his daughter spoke poked an anthill of emotions. "Miss Beth has no time for teaching."

"Yes, she does. She told me we could practice at her studio at Miss Francie's house."

He handed back her phone. "When did you talk to Beth?"

"Gram and I stopped in to see you after school

today, only you weren't there. I stayed and talked to her while Gram went to the bank."

Noah set his jaw. He'd have to have a talk with his grandmother. He didn't want Chloe getting too attached to Beth. Better yet, he'd have a talk with Beth himself and set her straight about a few things.

The next morning, Noah parked his car beside the small building behind the Montgomery home that had been converted into Beth's dance studio. Yesterday he'd been determined to tell Beth to back off and not mention dancing to Chloe. But he'd been unable to dismiss his gram's advice. Chloe was growing up, and she would strike out on her own. He didn't want her resenting him for denying her something she longed to do. But there was one other fact that wore away at his resentment. What if Gram was right, and Beth could never dance *en pointe* again?

He knew what it was like to have your dreams shattered and see the future you dreamed of go up in smoke. Beth must be suffering greatly with the prospect of never being a ballerina again. It had been her whole life.

He stepped inside the studio and found her on the small settee, her head resting on her knees. A twinge of concern hit him. As he approached, he saw her shoulder shake, which elevated his concern. "Beth, are you all right? Are you hurt?"

She jerked, lifting her head and blinking away tears. "Noah. What are you doing here?"

Taking a tissue from the box on the side table, she wiped her eyes, then rose to face him. His heart lodged in his throat. She was the essence of femininity. The black leotard and tights highlighted every feminine curve. The filmy overskirt that ended around her knees swished enticingly as she moved. Her dark hair, usually floating around her face, was pulled back into a haphazard knot at the back of her head. She looked every inch the professional ballerina—except for the sadness in her hazel eyes that brought an unfamiliar ache to his chest. He fought the sudden need to pull her close and comfort her. "You first. Why are you crying?"

She lifted her chin in a defiant gesture, only to sigh and lower her gaze, her fingers toying with strings on her skirt. "I was thinking about my daddy and how much I miss him. It's been a year already, and I still have this horrible hole in my heart."

It was not what he'd expected her to say, but he was very familiar with the emotion. "My gramps has been gone two years, and I still expect him to walk into the shop or come up behind me and squeeze my shoulder."

"Two years?" She gave him a sad smile. "I was hoping you'd say something to make me feel better." She glanced around the studio. "Daddy built this for me when I was ten. I'd told him that I was going to devote my life to dancing, and he said if that was true then I needed a place where I could practice every day."

"And you did." He remembered the hours she spent locked away. He'd count the minutes until she would step outside, put the practice behind her and become his friend. "I'm sure he was very proud of you."

She smiled, a sweet one this time that melted his insides. "He was. He never missed a performance, and he always gave me a bouquet of pink roses afterward no matter how small my part. I felt like a real princess.

He was my biggest fan." She met his gaze, then set her hands on her hips. "Your turn. Why are you here?"

The determination that had driven him here had been diluted by Beth's tears. Seeing her in her element, here in the studio, forced him to understand the significance of her loss. For all his issues with Beth, he would never want her to lose the thing she loved most. Gram was right. He couldn't control his daughter's dreams. Making too much of his disapproval might have the opposite effect. And in the short term, Beth would eventually leave, and by then Chloe would hopefully have moved on to a new interest.

"I came by to tell you that if you're still willing, I think adding dance along with Chloe's PT might be a good idea."

"Really? I'd love to. In fact, I'm going to start working with my niece and her friend. Chloe can join us, and we'll have a little dance class here. It should be fun."

Seeing the joy and anticipation on her face left a warm softness in his rib cage.

"What made you change your mind?"

He didn't realize how close they stood until he looked into her eyes. He could see the gold streak in the left one. "I can't say no to my little girl."

She chuckled softly and touched his arm. "Neither could my dad."

He looked into her eyes and saw them dilate. His pulse flipped. She was so close, he caught the flowery scent of her hair. He gathered himself and stepped back. She'd always made his heart race. Her loveliness never failed to captivate him, but she wasn't dependable. There was no room in her world for anyone else.

The frown on her face told him Beth clearly felt his withdrawal.

"You won't change your mind, will you? About Chloe I mean?"

He rubbed his forehead, already regretting his impulse. "No." Noah cleared his throat. "She needs to do her PT, and if dancing gets it done then I'm all for it." He pulled out a business card and handed it to her. "I have one request. Call Pete Jones, her physical therapist, and make sure you know what her parameters are and that he approves of whatever type of dancing you're planning."

"Of course. I'll be very cautious, Noah. You can depend on me."

That was the one thing he couldn't do. "Then I'll be going. Let me know when Chloe should be here."

She stared at him, a questioning look in her eyes. "Okay."

He held her gaze a moment before walking to the door. He had a bad feeling he'd just made a terrible mistake.

Chapter Three

The Sunday morning air was cool but pleasant for early November as Beth strolled through the courthouse park. Above the giant old magnolias and moss-draped live oaks, she could see the white steeple of Peace Community Church like a friendly hand beckoning her home. She'd agreed to meet her mother and family for late services today. She'd begged off her first two Sundays here, but she knew she couldn't do that any longer. Surprisingly, instead of dreading going to church, she found herself looking forward to it. She'd realized last night that worship had been one of the things missing in her life the last few years. She hadn't turned her back on God or lost her faith, but it had taken a seat high in the back balcony of her life to other things. It wasn't something she was proud of.

The front steps of the old brick church were crowded with members chatting and laughing. She wasn't in the mood to talk about her career or her reasons for being home. It was too painful a topic. Skirting the front entrance, she took the walkway along the side of the building and entered through one of the side doors. It didn't take long to find her family. They always sat midway up in the sanctuary. Her older brothers, Linc and Gil, were already seated with their wives and children. Her mother was talking to Evelyn Carlisle. Beth groaned inwardly, hoping they weren't talking about her. Too late. Her mother spotted her and waved her over.

"Beth, Evelyn tells me that she asked you to help with the Christmas show. That's a great idea. I think you should. It would be good for you to get involved."

The woman laid her hand on her heart. "You would be an answer to my prayers."

"What about my job with you?"

Her mom waved off her concerns. "Don't worry about that. I'm used to running my business alone."

Beth forced a smile. Evelyn and her mom had skillfully funneled her to a point where her only option was to say yes. "I'd love to help you out. When would you like me to start?"

Evelyn grinned. "Wonderful. We rehearse two nights a week and on Saturdays. We're having a board meeting at the theater Tuesday evening. Why don't you come, and I'll introduce you to everyone. Oh, and let's keep this between the two of us for the time being. I want it to be a surprise for the board."

The organ began to play softly, and Evelyn excused herself and moved off. Beth saw her stop at a pew near the front, where Noah and Chloe were seated. Noah glanced over his shoulder, and their eyes met. Her heart skipped a beat. For a moment she felt the old link between them. She wanted to go to him and ask him to help her sort out her life. But he looked away, leaving her adrift again. She had the horrible feeling that he would never forgive her for leaving the way she had. She wasn't sure she could live with that fact, because despite the years and the distance, she still cared for him. He was the best friend she'd ever had, the only person who understood her. She couldn't make that go away.

Beth forced thoughts of Noah and the past out of her mind, suddenly craving the comfort and peace she'd always found in the historic church. In her drive to reach the top of her profession, she'd lost that feeling. She was beginning to think she'd lost far more than an active faith life.

Despite her best efforts, her mind wandered through the early parts of the service. Her gaze drifted to Noah, then to her brothers. Gil had his arm draped across the back of the pew, wrapping Julie in a subtle hug. Linc held Gemma's hand, which was resting on his thigh.

A surge of longing swelled from deep inside. She wanted that kind of connection. A hand to hold, someone to depend on. For the last twelve years it had been her career, but that had failed her and set her adrift in a world she no longer knew how to navigate.

Reverend Jim Barrett's gravelly voice pulled her from her negative thoughts.

"The first commandment is 'You shall have no other Gods before Me.' Have you considered how hard it is to follow? It's the most important of the ten, but we treat it lightly. What God have you set in place of the Lord? What goal, passion, hobby or desire have you, unintentionally probably, set in place of God? What is it that you work harder for, strive for, push everything and everyone else aside for to achieve?"

A warm rush heated Beth's cheeks, making her

squirm. Was he talking to her? Had he known she would be here today?

"I know we all have to do certain things to meet our goals to get that promotion or earn that raise. We tell ourselves it's so we can provide a better life for our family or for ourselves. But the problem lies in the definition of better life. If you're ignoring your family, your friends and your God, then how can that make anything better? Ask yourself what is your goal really costing you? People, jobs, dreams will all fail you. Put Him first always, and He'll take care of the rest."

Beth stood for the final hymn, her mind replaying the things she'd heard. Had she done that? Had she pushed aside those she loved in her drive to achieve her lifelong dream? The answer wasn't hard to find. She had. A sour feeling formed in her stomach. The buzz and push of people making their way out of the sanctuary pressed in on her. Her mother was talking to a friend. Her brothers and their families had exited the pew on the other end, leaving her a clear path to the side door. Quickly she made her way to the side aisle, but before she could reach the door she heard her name called. Chloe hurried toward her.

"Daddy says I can take dancing lessons from you. When can I come?"

Noah stepped forward, resting his hands on his daughter's shoulders and looking absurdly handsome in a dark suit and crisp white shirt that contrasted pleasantly with his sun-darkened skin. The sky blue tie lying against his chest made his eyes even bluer. But the deep scowl on his face said he still had strong reservations about the situation.

Ignoring the wince of discomfort his look caused,

she looked at Chloe. "I was thinking we'd meet twice a week on Tuesdays and Thursdays, right after school."

Chloe frowned. "Not every day?"

"No, that's not good for your muscles when you're starting out. Even I have to take some downtime. And I have a surprise for you. My niece Abby and her friend Hannah are going to come, too."

"Really? Cool. Abby's here today. Dad, can I go find her?"

He nodded, giving her a loving smile before turning his blue eyes on her. She knew exactly what he was going to say. "Yes, I spoke with Pete and he's all for the ballet lessons with a few exceptions. But those are things she wouldn't be learning for a few months anyway."

"What time will the lessons be? I need to work it into my schedule."

"You plan on watching the entire hour?"

"Yes."

"I wish you wouldn't. It's not good for Chloe if you're hovering all the time."

"I want to make sure nothing happens."

Evelyn joined them, giving her grandson a light swat on his shoulder. "Noah, stop behaving like an overprotective father. Beth is a professional, and I'm quite certain she knows what she's doing."

Beth stifled a smile at the resigned look on Noah's face. "Thank you, Miss Evelyn, for the vote of confidence. I'll take good care of all the girls."

Noah set his jaw and made an excuse to leave. After he stepped away, Evelyn slipped her arm in Beth's and walked her toward the side door.

Evelyn pulled her a little closer. "We have some

things to discuss, dear, and now that you're part of the little theater we'll have plenty of time to catch up."

Beth wasn't sure what she meant exactly, but she liked the idea. She had a feeling there was a lot more to Noah's attitude than she knew. They'd been close back then, and she'd been able to sense his moods—except for the day she'd given him his graduation gift and he'd handed it back. Figuratively, of course. She had to find out why he was still holding an old grudge.

Maybe by accepting Evelyn's offer, she could learn more about Noah's attitude and find a way to repair the damage from the past.

Beth couldn't remember the last time she'd been this anxious about anything. Not even her first solo performance as principal ballerina had tied her stomach in this many twisted knots. She scanned her small studio again. It was cleaned up and ready for her first students. Abby, Hannah and Chloe would be arriving soon for their first class.

Beth had conferred with Pete Jones a few more times about things she wanted to teach to make sure she fully understood Chloe's condition. He'd offered to work with her, too, if she needed any help with her ACL rehab.

She exhaled a long sigh, clasped her hands together and glanced for the tenth time at the clock, fighting the churning sensation inside. For most of her dancing career she'd been the student, attending daily classes and rehearsals. She'd helped other dancers in her career, but they'd been professionals seeking advice. She'd never taught beginners, especially children. What if she was too technical? What if she pushed too hard or became impatient? What if—

"Aunt Beth, they're here." Abby charged through the door, all smiles.

"Hi, Miss Beth." Chloe followed behind, and Hannah brought up the rear.

"Hello, ladies. You look excited."

Hannah giggled. "We're not ladies. We're girls."

Beth tapped her shoulder. "You are young ladies who are going to learn the first few positions of ballet."

Chloe clapped her hands. "On our toes?"

"Not yet. You have to work up to that. Put your things over there and we'll get started."

Beth's new sister-in-law, Julie, stopped at her side. "Thank you for doing this. Abby and Hannah were so excited on the way over, I thought my eardrums would burst."

"I have to admit I was nervous about this at first, but I think it'll be fun."

"And much needed."

"What do you mean?"

"Abby has wanted to take dancing for a while, but the only school near here is in Sawyer's Bend. I've been reluctant to let her attend there. I've heard some disturbing things about the kind of dance moves they teach."

Beth looked to her sister-in-law for an explanation.

"A lot of the moms here in Dover have pulled their girls from that school. At the last recital Hannah was in, she looked like a pole dancer. Her mother was furious."

Beth was well aware of the suggestive movements popular in today's world, though she couldn't imagine teaching some of them to children. "I had no idea that was happening."

"How do you teach your daughter Christian values and modesty when the world tells them it's okay to dance like a stripper? Maybe you should think about opening up a school here. I know dozens of mothers would love to sign their children up if they knew they didn't have to worry about inappropriate dances."

Julie waved goodbye, and Beth focused her attention on her students. But her sister-in-law's suggestion began to churn in the back of her mind.

"Okay, ladies, let's get started. First we have to stretch out all our muscles."

She noted with interest what each girl had decided to wear. Abby had chosen black tights, leather dance flats and a purple-and-black leotard. Hannah wore bike shorts and a tank top. Chloe proudly wore traditional pink tights and a leotard with a net tutu to match.

Hannah chuckled. "You don't need a tutu to practice, silly."

"I don't care. I want to look like Miss Beth, and that means I have to have a tutu."

"But she's not wearing a tutu today," Abby pointed out.

Beth chuckled and gestured to her all-black dance ensemble with a knee-length wrap skirt.

"You wear what makes you comfortable. And today I'm comfortable looking like a teacher. First we warm up."

Watching the girls' excitement as she introduced simple steps and explained various movements chased away her lingering nerves. They were sweet and eager to learn. She'd take her cues from them and use this first class as her barometer to gauge how she would proceed.

An hour later the girls were pulling on their jackets and gathering up their things. The warm glow filling her chest as she watched them brought a smile to her face. Teaching these girls had been more enjoyable than she'd ever expected. Their energy and enthusiasm had filled her with joy. The idea of a dance school didn't seem like the end of the road, but a possible new bend in it.

Abby and Hannah waved and hurried out the door. Chloe stood at the barre pretending to be on her toes as she waited for her father to pick her up. A flash of light and a soft squeak filled the studio as the door opened and Noah strode in. In his leather jacket, which showed off the breadth of his shoulders, and faded jeans that hugged his muscular legs, he bore little resemblance to the tall, skinny boy she remembered. He grinned in her direction, his blue eyes soft with affection. Her pulse hiccupped. It quickly stilled when she realized his warm welcome was directed at his daughter and not her.

Chloe ran toward him and gave him a quick hug, chattering about what she'd learned. He gave Chloe a pat on the shoulder. "I'm glad you had fun. Why don't you wait in the car? I want to talk to Miss Beth for a second. I'll be right there."

Chloe waved and smiled before walking outside.

Noah finally settled his clear blue gaze on her, and her pulse jumped again. Something in his attitude raised her defenses. "She did very well. In fact, I know you don't want to hear this, but she's a natural. I don't think you'll have any problem getting her to do her exercises now."

"That's good. I just want to make sure she doesn't get any ideas when it comes to these dance classes. I don't want you glamorizing your profession, making it appear all fun and games."

Beth set her jaw and crossed her arms over her chest. "I will always answer her questions honestly. I won't sugarcoat anything, but I won't lie about the enjoyment and satisfaction, either."

"I don't want her lured into thinking fame is something she should chase after. It only leads to disappointment and ruins relationships."

She shook her head. "I never chased the fame, Noah. You know that."

A muscle flexed in his jaw, and his eyes narrowed. "Not you. Her mother. How can a husband and child compete with Hollywood celebrity?"

Stunned, Beth could only watch as he spun around and walked out. Had his wife walked out on him and Chloe? She knew he was divorced, but she'd never thought about what had brought it about. Is that why he was so against anything connected to the arts? It explained a lot. She wanted to ask him what had happened, to help her understand his animosity. Hurrying to the door, she opened it as his car disappeared around the bend in the drive.

This is what had been the strength of their relationship—the ability to help each other through hard times. Noah needed someone to talk to, to work out his anger. It wasn't all about her after all. He'd been hurt deeply by his wife's betrayal.

But first they had to get beyond their own past.

* * *

Noah tried to pay attention to the conversation going on between his gram and Chloe as they ate supper that evening, but they were talking about Beth, the last thing he wanted to hear. He was trying not to think of her, but he'd found that to be difficult. Gram had fixed his favorite—roast beef with homemade noodles—but he was barely aware of eating any.

He blinked and tried to pick up the thread of the conversation. He knew it had something to do with the first dance class earlier today, but all he could think about was the joy on Beth's face when he entered the studio. Chloe had been bubbling over with excitement, but Beth's expression was one of pure delight. Her hazel eyes had sparkled, and her smile was brighter than morning sunshine. He'd been caught off guard by the emotions swirling up from deep inside. All his old feelings came roaring back. He'd reacted by blurting out the truth about Yvonne. He hadn't intended to, but sharing his concerns with her was as natural as breathing.

He'd forced himself to listen to Chloe and keep his eyes away from Beth. He'd slammed his defenses into place. He couldn't forget that she was driven and focused and had only one agenda in her life. One that didn't include family and friends.

"Noah. Noah. Yoo-hoo."

He jerked his head up. Gram was staring at him. "Sorry. I was thinking about…work. What were you saying?"

Gram peered over her glasses. "I was reminding you that there's a board meeting for the little theater this evening. Your presence is required."

Chloe groaned. "Does that mean I have to go, too? Those meetings are boring."

"Maybe so, but you can't stay here all alone. You can use my tablet while you wait."

A mischievous grin appeared on her face, putting a sparkle in her eyes. "Can I watch videos of Miss Beth?"

He still didn't like the idea. The more she watched the clips, the more time she spent with Beth, the greater the risk of her latching on to a dream that could only bring heartache and disappointment. But he couldn't keep her a baby forever. "Okay, but I'm going to put your spelling words and your study guide for the test on Friday on there, too, so you can spend part of the time looking at those."

A half hour later he pulled out of the drive for the short trip to the little theater. For a man who vowed to steer clear of any artistic endeavors, he found himself hip-deep in them. First his gram sweet-talks him into taking part in her renewed theater project, then Beth comes back to town and gets Chloe involved in dance classes.

He really needed a nice steel rod to insert into his spine. Either that, or he had too many women in his life. Problem was he loved them too much to turn down their pleas for help.

Except Beth. He couldn't deny he felt something, but he was absolutely sure it had nothing at all to do with love. It was merely an emotional muscle memory being reawakened. It would settle back down soon enough.

Noah opened the back door of the old building to allow his gram and Chloe to enter. The board usually met in a small room at the back. He never had much to add to the proceedings. His lack of creativity put him at odds with the other members, and only reminded him of high school and being the misfit. The only time he'd felt he belonged was when he'd become friends with Beth. But he did it to please his gram, and he tried to act as the practical, business-minded member.

He stepped into the cramped space and froze.

"Miss Beth." Chloe darted between the members and into Beth's arms.

Noah stared at Beth, his emotions tilting between surprise and dread. What was she doing here?

His gram hurried toward Beth, too, patting her cheek and smiling before directing her to be seated. In his stunned state, he waited too long to choose a seat and ended up having to take the chair next to Beth. He leaned toward her slightly. "Why are you here?"

"I'm taking Allison's place. You?"

"I'm on the board." She met his gaze with an insincere smile that created a kink in his chest.

Gram was sorting through her papers, and Chloe had curled up in a chair in the corner, busily tapping away on his tablet. He had a feeling she was watching videos of Beth again.

"Good evening, ladies and gentlemen. We have some new business to go over, and I want to get right to it before we address the other issues. Beth, my dear, would you stand?"

Her chair squeaked as she moved to rise, and Noah reached for the back to pull it away.

He didn't want to look at her, but he couldn't help it. Her smile was warm and genuine now as she touched each member with her gaze.

"I'd like you to meet our new dance coordinator, Miss Bethany Montgomery. I'm sure you all know some member of the Montgomery family. There are a bunch of them here in Dover." She paused as the members chuckled. "And you may know that Beth is a professional ballerina. She's home now and has graciously agreed to take Allison's place."

His gaze traveled around the room as the board gave Beth a round of polite applause. Gram looked delighted. Smug, actually, which raised a flag in the back of his mind. She then introduced the other board members: Shelby Durrant, who owned a small stationery shop on the square, Todd Newsome, the new president of the bank and David Atkins, an attorney.

"I'm sure her knowledge and expertise will add another level of excitement to our humble production," Gram said after she had introduced everyone and turned back to Beth.

"Thank you all," Beth said. "I'm looking forward to being a part of the *Christmas Dreams* musical."

"Noah, dear. Why don't you show Bethany around and introduce her to everyone. I'll fill you in on our discussions later."

Trapped, he had no recourse but to agree. With a stiff smile and a wave of his hand, he gestured her to precede him. Once outside the small room, he stopped, only to have Chloe bump into him from behind. "Where are you going?"

"I want to look around, too."

"Not happening." He took her hand and marched her to the steps along the side of the stage. "See those nice comfy seats? Pick one, open your homework and get busy."

With a barely stifled groan, a roll of her big blue eyes and a dejected droop to her shoulders, she stomped down the wooden steps and threw herself into a seat, scowling at him above the tablet. Anticipating her next comment, he pointed at her. "Homework. No videos." It earned him another glare.

A soft snicker to his left drew his attention. Beth was covering her mouth with her fingertips, her eyes bursting with amusement. "What?"

"I thought you said you couldn't say no to your little girl?"

"Not all the time." He faced her. "What changed your mind?"

"I missed the theater. I thought it would be good to help out and keep busy."

"You don't have enough to do with working for your mom and teaching dancing?"

"Teaching only takes two hours a week. And I don't work full-time at the office. That leaves a lot of free time. Even with daily workouts."

"So what happens to this show when you're all healed up and you run back to New York?"

The teasing smile that had lit her eyes suddenly vanished, and the hazel color shifted into the dark brown spectrum. "I'm not going anywhere for a long time. I have three, maybe four months of rehab yet to do before I'll be cleared to dance, so you can stop stressing over that. I'll be here to finish the performance."

"Good, because it would break Gram's heart if you just disappeared one day."

"Noah, I left here suddenly because an incredible opportunity came my way. I apologize for not keeping in touch afterward, but frankly, I didn't think you'd care one way or the other. You transferred to another college and got married. Your life went in a different direction. So did mine."

Why would she think he hadn't cared? He opened his mouth to ask when someone tapped his shoulder. He glanced around to see the director of the show at his side.

"Is this our new dance teacher?" She gasped, before letting out a high-pitched squeal. What was it with women that they had to screech when they were happy? Chloe did it all the time.

"Beth Montgomery. Please tell me you're replacing Allison."

"Jenny Olsen. Oh, it's so good to see you. Yes, I am. You?"

She held out her arms. "I'm the director of this extravaganza."

Noah tamped down his irritation while the women went through another round of squeals and giggles. He'd forgotten that Jen and Beth had been friends since grade school. As soon as he could get a word in, he made his escape. "Now that you two have been reunited, I'm going to get back to the board meeting. Jen, I'm sure you can give Beth the tour."

Jen linked arms with her old friend and waved him away. "I'd love to."

He watched as the women walked off, knowing his Plan A to keep his distance from Beth was toast. Beth glanced over her shoulder at him, a taunting smile on her face. She was enjoying his discomfort, and he had his gram to thank for this. Pivoting, he started back to the stage, pausing only to remind his daughter to finish her homework.

He had to come up with a Plan B. Fast. He was already having a hard time with Beth working next door. Now he'd have to deal with her at the theater for the next several weeks, as well. Maybe she'd leave soon.

No. Then the show would suffer. And Chloe would be upset.

Rubbing his forehead, he sent up a prayer for strength and guidance in dealing with the three females complicating his life.

Chapter Four

Beth moved to the large mirror leaning against the wall in her bedroom, taking a few deep breaths. Tonight would be her first rehearsal for the Christmas show, and she wanted to make a good impression so she'd pulled on her best dark jeans, low-heeled boots that ended right above her ankles and a sophisticated dark green cowl-necked jersey top with a diagonal insert.

She frowned at her reflection. She was overdressed for a little theater practice. Tugging off the tunic, she slipped on a simple gray crew neck sweater and draped a loop scarf over her head. Better. At least in Mississippi she didn't have to wear a bulky winter coat and hat. Clothes usually gave her confidence. Not tonight. Now she was wishing she'd thought things through more.

Learning Noah was on the board of directors of the little theater had challenged her decision. Judging from his expression when he'd walked into the room, he'd been blindsided, too. She grinned as she remembered the look on his face, like a man who'd been dumped in the lake and suddenly realized he couldn't swim.

She was treading water, as well. The more she was near him and the more they talked, the more she remembered how much his friendship mattered, and how he'd given her a sense of belonging she'd always missed. As much as her family loved her, and she had no doubts that they did, she'd always felt different. Her siblings were all extroverts—she was the only introvert in the clan. Noah had made her feel that being different was the perfect way for her to be.

Taking a deep breath, she put on her earrings and squared her shoulders. How bad could it be? It's not as if Noah was involved with the production. Besides, in a few weeks it would be over, and she needed something to fill her time beyond working in the real estate office. Once she got past this first meeting, everything would be fine.

Her gaze landed on her tablet as she reached for her purse, sending a thread of shame through her mind. Noah's comment about his divorce had spurred her curiosity. She'd caved to temptation and looked up Noah's wife online. Apparently the stunning blonde had exploded on the news scene like a rocket, going from weekend reporter on a network affiliate to being an anchor to having her own talk show in less than three years. What had disturbed her, however, was that there was no mention of a husband or a child in her bio, only the celebrity aspects of her life. No wonder Noah was so against Chloe getting ideas about anything concerning performing. He was probably afraid Chloe would want to follow in her mother's footsteps.

Noah was a black-and-white thinker, and knowing

him, he'd obviously equated her leaving to become a professional ballerina with his wife doing the same to become a TV personality and concluded that keeping Chloe away from the arts was keeping her from heartbreak. But that didn't fully explain why he was so angry with her. She hadn't left a husband and child behind.

She locked the door and dropped the key into her bag, striding down the sidewalk along Main Street. The little theater was only a block off Peace Street, an easy walk from her apartment. The parking lot was full when she arrived. Making her way up the concrete steps at the back of the old two-story brick building, she stepped inside and her concerns melted away. This was her world. She took a deep breath and went in search of Jen.

Shorty Zimmerman, the theater manager and insurance agent, informed her Jen was backstage. Beth made her way down the aisles, taking time to appreciate the surroundings. She'd been too busy meeting cast and crew the other night. The theater looked the same as she remembered. Old, small and in need of major remodeling. It wasn't designed as a theater originally. It had been coaxed into the role with leftover seating and other materials from a variety of sources, one of which was the old Palace movie theater on Church Street. She hated to think of that grand old structure decaying away, but no one had stepped up to preserve it. Supposedly a full restoration was too expensive. Not to mention Dutch Ingles owned it and the building next door, and the old miser refused to sell or donate the theater. But old or new, a theater had a certain atmosphere about it that revved up her excitement.

Jen hurried toward her. "Are you ready for this madness?"

"I think so."

"It'll be fun. You'll see." She handed her a piece of paper. "This is our program. Three acts. The first focuses on the secular aspect of Christmas—pop songs, presents and the like. Act two is family-oriented, with carols, a short scene from *The Nutcracker* and 'White Christmas.' Act three is about the real reason for the season—hymns, a nativity and a scripture reading."

"It sounds wonderful. You've included something for everyone."

"Beth." Jen touched her arm gently. "I didn't have a chance to mention it the other night, but I heard about your injury. I'm sorry. I know how much dancing has always meant to you."

Beth's heart swelled with warm affection. It would be good to have a friend to talk to. She hadn't realized how much she missed that. "Thank you. It's been a long, painful recovery."

"Do you think you'll be able to go back to ballet?"

A few days ago she would have snapped out a firm yes, but at the moment that seemed more like a hope than a certainty. "I'm not sure."

"Well, if anyone can make a comeback, it's you. You're the most committed, dedicated person I've ever known."

"I have to admit I'm nervous about this rehearsal."

"Don't be. Everyone here is sweet and eager to please. They are looking forward to working with you. Allison designed the dance numbers and the costumes, and everyone has learned their steps. Basically you'll just have to oversee rehearsals and keep them on track until the show. I think for tonight you can just find a seat, watch the numbers and then we'll go over any questions or concerns you might have."

Jen's enthusiasm lightened Beth's mood as she found a seat in the sixth row, where she could see the entire stage. Pulling out her tablet, she swiped to the note app and turned her full attention to the performers.

The numbers were charming and engaging, but she saw room for improvement both in the dances and the scenery. With a little effort she could easily bump up the show to another level and make it sparkle. She wasn't sure how Jen would take to her ideas, though.

When the rehearsal was over, Jen motioned Beth forward and introduced her to the cast. Beth made the appropriate speech of reassurance and encouragement.

Jen dismissed everyone then faced her. "Did you have any suggestions or questions about the numbers? I saw you making notes."

"I do." Beth ran through some of her thoughts about changes to the choreography and expanding the scenes to amp up the excitement. Jen nodded thoughtfully, and Beth braced herself for pushback. She didn't want to complicate things. She was here to help and not to cause trouble. If Jen didn't agree with her suggestions, then she'd leave things as is.

Her friend released a long, slow sigh. "I'm so glad you said that. Allison did her best, but I felt the numbers lacked that element of excitement. They seemed flat and boring to me. Do you think you can fix them?"

Relief and anticipation swirled inside her chest. "I believe I can. Do you have the time and money to add to the sets and maybe a few new costumes?"

"Absolutely. Miss Evelyn is fully committed to this

show, so money isn't an issue. We can certainly add to the sets if our carpenter has time. We won't rehearse over Thanksgiving, so that leaves only three weeks until we open." She pulled out her phone and typed in a text message. "I love your ideas, Beth. I think you're exactly what we needed for this production. We all want it to be a worthy addition to the holiday celebrations. I know we're all amateurs, but I'd like this to be as professional as possible."

"Hey, Jen, what's up?"

Beth spun around at the sound of Noah's smooth voice. "What are you doing here?"

Jen glanced at her. "Oh, didn't I tell you? Noah is our set builder. Anything you want constructed for the numbers, he'll make it happen."

Beth wasn't sure how she felt about that. Being around Noah was already stirring old emotions. She didn't need any more exposure to this new, compelling version of her old friend. "I'd forgotten you were handy with a hammer."

"Thanks to the insistence of my grandpa." He raised an eyebrow, and his blue eyes held a challenge. "I'm the go-to guy. Whatever you need built, fixed or scrounged up, I'm the one to call."

"Beth has some ideas to spruce up the show, and she might need a few props built."

Noah looked like he'd sooner swallow nails. "Give me a sketch, and I'll see what I can do."

Jen was called away for a phone call, leaving them alone, a painfully awkward silence hanging between them, like actors who had forgotten their lines. If her presence here was going to create tension, then maybe she should bow out. "I had no idea you were so involved in this production."

"Like I said, it's hard to say no to the women in my life. Gram asked me to help out."

"If this is going to be uncomfortable, I'll quit."

Noah looked surprised. "I never said that. I'm sure the show will benefit from your knowledge and experience."

The performers had drifted out, and the stagehands were putting their gear away. When the bank of lights over the stage shut down, Beth draped her purse over her shoulder. "That's our cue to leave. Say hello to Chloe for me."

"Sure." They walked to the back door, exiting with a few stragglers. After saying good-night to Shorty, they stepped out into the small parking lot. Beth searched for something to say. "It was like old times. We helped your gram with a couple little theater shows, as I recall."

Noah shoved his hands into his jacket pockets and rocked back on his heels. "That was a long time ago."

He was shutting her out. It was a feeling she was well acquainted with. Being different. Not being included in groups. But it had been Noah who'd given her a place to belong. They'd both been oddballs; it's why they'd grown so close. But now *he* was the one closing the door.

She blinked and turned away, not wanting him to see how hurt she was. "Yes, it was. Good night."

Folding her arms around her waist to ward off the night chill, she started toward home. Would she always feel like the outsider? The one who didn't fit? Not with her family, not with her school friends, not even with her coworkers. The only place she fit was on stage. And that was closed to her now, as well.

Noah watched Beth walk across the parking lot and down the sidewalk toward her apartment. He'd caught a glimpse of the moisture in her eyes, and he'd quickly regretted his harsh words. Being close to Beth brought out the worst in him. She'd stepped in to help, and he'd behaved like an ungrateful jerk. A quick glance around the deserted street raised his concern. It was a full block to the town square, and the building where she lived stood at the far end. He couldn't in all good conscience let her walk alone. After tossing his things into the back of his car, he jogged to catch up with her. "Hey. You shouldn't walk home alone."

She stopped and faced him. The light spilling from the corner streetlamp danced on her dark hair and made her eyes shine.

"It's only a block, and there are plenty of street-lights." She pointed to the one on the edge of the square. "Besides, Dover is the safest place on earth."

"Maybe, but I think I'd better see you home."

She chuckled. The sound washed through him like sparkling water.

"You sound so formal and polite. Evelyn would be pleased. But seriously, I'll be fine."

Noah took her arm and steered her forward. "Nope. I want to make sure you get home safely."

"Thank you."

They walked in silence, and Noah searched for a topic that didn't touch on their past. Sadly, there were none he wanted to bring up. Finally Beth spoke.

"I have a confession to make. I looked up your former wife on the internet."

He wasn't surprised. He knew she'd be curious. "No problem. I looked you up, too."

He'd learned enough about ACL reconstruction to know that Beth's dream of returning to dancing was a slim one.

"You did?"

"Chloe wanted to see some videos of you performing."

"Oh." She sounded disappointed.

"I didn't realize how serious your injury was. I'm sorry."

"Thanks. Other dancers have made a successful comeback. I could, too. I don't give up easily."

"I remember." Nothing came between her and her desire to dance. "Did you find all the answers to your questions about Yvonne?"

"Some. What disturbed me was that there was no mention of a husband and child in her bio."

A strangled chuckle escaped his throat before he could stop it. "That's because a family didn't fit with her image. Her manager wanted to present her as free and unencumbered."

"I'm surprised she agreed to that. It seems so cold and heartless." She stopped. "I'm sorry. That was a very thoughtless thing to say."

He looked at Beth. Even in the faint light, her hazel eyes were filled with sympathy. The Beth he remembered, even when obsessed with her dancing, had carried a heart for others. For the first time, he wondered if perhaps she still existed beneath the professional drive. He hoped so. He'd like to spend time with her again.

"But true. She wasn't always like that. We met in college my sophomore year. She wasn't like anyone I'd ever met. She was outrageous, impulsive and exciting. She showed me a way of life I'd never known before. I was looking to make a change, and she made it happen."

The boy he'd been hadn't been enough for Beth, so he'd decided to reinvent himself, and Yvonne had been his teacher. Yvonne had changed the outside of him. She'd encouraged him to work out, taught him how to present himself. She'd given him a total makeover, down to hairstyle and wardrobe. Unfortunately, clothes could only make the man to a point. While he looked confident and polished on the outside, on the inside he was still the same misfit with thick glasses who never belonged. Except with Beth.

"She sounds amazing."

"It all happened fast. We fell in love, got married and then Chloe came along. Everything seemed possible. We were going to school, working and raising our daughter. After graduation, she got an offer from a big network affiliate in San Francisco, and I hired on with a prestigious engineering firm. All our dreams were coming true."

"Then her career took off?"

He nodded. "An overnight sensation."

"And she just left? How could she do that?"

"I believe her reasoning was that she couldn't make us happy if she didn't first make herself happy."

Beth slipped her hand in his, sending a jolt along his senses. He told himself to pull away, but her fingers felt good entwined with his. The old habit of baring his soul to her took over. "Truth is, she left long before she walked out the door. I stayed in San Francisco so Chloe could see her mother from time to time, but those times eventually became never. When Gram got sick last spring, I decided to come back home."

"Chloe told me her mother is going to send her a plane ticket to visit for Thanksgiving."

Noah shook his head. "Never going to happen. She makes plans with Chloe all the time that she never keeps."

"Poor baby."

"Chloe keeps dreaming that one day her mom will come and get her, and they'll go on wonderful adventures together."

"Is that why you don't want her to dream? Because dreams don't always come true?"

"Dreams set you up for heartbreak." He could sense Beth gearing up for an argument, and he was thankful that they'd reached the apartment. He waited while she fished out her key and unlocked the door.

"Thank you for walking me home. You were always such a gentleman. It was one of the things I liked most about you."

He wanted to ask if there had been other things she liked, but thought better of the idea. "Thank my gram. Any good manners I possess are her doing."

"Good night, Noah. Be careful walking back to the theater."

He grinned and held up his arm, flexing the muscle. "Never fear. I can handle it." That earned him a bright smile. He walked away, acutely aware of Beth's eyes on his back. He took his time walking down Main Street. Dover at this time of night was quiet and still, and he let the peacefulness ease some of his concerns. The tension between the two of them had been uncomfortable. But like it or not, he'd have to work with her for the next several weeks. He'd given his commitment to helping his gram with her dream, and he wouldn't let her down.

The hair on the back of his neck tingled and he stopped, cautiously glancing around. Was someone watching him? Slowly he scanned the darkened storefronts, the shadowed paths through the park. He looked behind him and his gaze traveled to the balcony above his office, the one in Beth's apartment. He saw her, leaning over the iron railing, her head sticking out from behind one of the vine-covered posts. He started to raise his hand, but looked away and started walking again.

Why was she watching him? To make sure he reached the theater safely? Or was there something more?

Beth took the hand of her older brother, Gil, seated to her right, and the smaller hand of her niece Abby on her left. Closing her eyes, she listened to the soft tone of her mother's voice as she offered grace over the meal. Her mind filled with a rush of memories of family dinners here in the old house. Back then it had been her father saying the blessing, his deep voice strong and reverent, giving thanks for all they had and for each other. The memory filled her with familiar warmth and a deep, aching sadness. Even after a year, her father's presence lingered within the walls. It probably always would.

Beth ate in silence, letting the chatter of her family fill the air. Linc and Gil were each happily married to wonderful women. Linc and Gemma were expecting their first child. Beth had bonded with her new sisters-in-law quickly, and she found her new nephew, Evan, a joy. Having her niece, Abby, back in the family was another blessing. Her family had grown in the last year. Everything was changing—in her world, too.

After dinner Beth joined her mother in the kitchen to clean up.

"So, how are things going with you and Noah? Are you getting caught up?"

"Not really. I don't think he's interested in catching up."

"Why?"

She shrugged. "He's angry with me for not staying in touch, which doesn't make sense because he didn't stay in touch with me, either."

"You did leave suddenly." She shook her head. "That was a crazy time."

"Even crazier when I got up there. I remember waking up one day, and it was September and I had no idea where the summer had gone."

Mom nodded, folding the dish towel slowly. "You went from amateur to professional literally overnight. That's a huge life change."

"That's what I told him, but he was upset that he had to learn about my job with Forsythe from the *Dover Dispatch* and not me."

"He was your closest friend. I would have thought you'd have found time to share your good news with him. It's important to stay in touch with loved ones."

The melancholy tone in her mom's voice tugged at her heart. "I stayed in touch. I called. I came home."

Her mother took a long moment to reply. "It would

have been nice to hear from you more often. I understood that your life would be hectic, and I knew you had to devote all your efforts toward succeeding, but your dad and I missed you. We felt a little abandoned at times."

Beth flipped back through her memory, sorting through the years. She could see now where she'd kept putting off coming home to visit, postponing phone calls. "I didn't intentionally cut you out of my life, Mom. Honest."

"I know, but it reached a point where the only time we heard from you was when you told us about your next performance. All I'm saying is that I can understand Noah's position."

Why did everyone blame her for not staying in touch? "The phone rings both ways."

"Yes, it does. I'm sorry if I sounded judgmental. Since your father has been gone, I do a lot of thinking back on things I wish I'd done differently. It's been a difficult year."

Beth moved to the window and stared outside, avoiding eye contact with her mother and hoping the subject was closed. The last few years of her life had been difficult for her as well, but she couldn't share the reasons with her mother. Not yet anyway.

"I'm glad you decided to help with the Christmas show. Now you can stop trying to stay in dancing form and focus on something else. Who knows. It might be the beginning of a whole new career for you."

Her mother's comment had stirred a dark pool of anger and grief. "Mom, I know you mean well, but you don't understand. Dancing has been my life since I was five. It's what I love. It's the most important aspect of who I am. You don't know what it's like to lose the thing that gives your life meaning and purpose."

Her mom came and took her hand, pulling her down beside her on the little bench beneath the window. "Bethany, I know better than anyone what you're going through. I've lost the person who gave my life meaning and purpose, the man I shared my life with and the father of my children. We were supposed to grow old together. We were going to travel and do all the things we couldn't do with five children. Now I'm struggling to learn to live alone, and figure out who I am without him by my side. It's hard, Bethany. It's painful. Some days I don't even want to get out of bed. But I can't shut down. I have to move forward no matter how difficult it is."

Beth's chest ached, and she swiped tears from her face. How could she have been so thoughtless and cruel? She'd been so focused on her own pain, she'd become blind to anyone else's. "Mama, I'm so sorry. I didn't mean to hurt you." A sob made its way up her throat. "I'm sorry." Her mother pulled her into her arms before she could move.

"I know. I understand how devastating this situation is for you, but we'll get through it. Together." She pulled a napkin from the table and gently dabbed at the tears on Beth's cheeks. "You're so much like your father. Strong, determined and fully committed to whatever goal you set. But sometimes that commitment makes it hard for you to see when it's time to let go."

"Is that even possible?"

"Not entirely. But when I look around at what the Lord has added to my life after losing your father, I have to be in awe of His blessing. In the last year Gil brought Abby home to us and added Julie to the family. Linc gave me Evan and Gemma." She brushed the hair off Beth's forehead. "And I have my little dancer back home again. If you let Him, the Lord will open new paths for you. But you have to let go."

With her throat tight with remorse and sadness, all she could do was nod. Her mother was right. She had to accept the truth and let go. But she had no idea how to do that. What if she let go, and there was nothing out there to grab hold of?

Chapter Five

Beth took her time walking to rehearsal Thursday night. She'd forgotten how pleasant November could be in Mississippi. She needed only a light jacket to protect from the cool wind. Back in New York, she'd be bundling up and digging out gloves and boots.

Nervous excitement bubbled in her rib cage as she neared the little theater, but her confidence ebbed and flowed. With the aid of videos of the performances Jen had sent her, she'd worked up simple steps and movements that would enhance each number. She hoped the dancers could pick up the changes quickly and wouldn't find the routines too complicated.

Her nervousness vanished over the next hour when the cast welcomed the additions she'd created. They admitted that Allison's routines were too simple, and they were eager to learn more to make the show better. After working out a new rehearsal schedule for each cast, she went in search of Noah to discuss her ideas for new props.

Other than a glimpse of him coming and going in the office, she hadn't seen him since he'd walked her home the other night, and she hadn't been able to get the incident out of her mind. His concern for her safety had shifted something inside her. She understood he was just being a gentleman, but there'd been something romantic about walking beside him along the dimly lit streets and saying good-night at her door. She groaned inwardly. Hadn't she learned the hard way that romantic gestures were worthless?

Learning about Noah's wife had given her insight into his attitude and his heart. Noah was a family man, a man who planted his roots deep into the ground. He'd spoken often about his parents and how someday he wanted to have a family of his own so he could recreate the happy life he'd known before their deaths.

In a way, they were very much alike. She was determined to excel in her career, and Noah was unshakable in his desire to provide a solid foundation for his daughter, even staying in San Francisco in an impossible situation for his daughter's sake. He'd moved home to help his gram. He was an admirable man, a man who would do anything for those he loved. But if betrayed, he would be a hard man to deal with.

She found Noah in the back of the building, talking with Shorty. He smiled when he saw her. The first genuine smile he'd given her since she'd seen him again. The way his lips tugged to one side when he smiled sent a trickle of warm appreciation along her nerves. His smile hadn't changed one bit, but the body around it had. *Gangly* had been a good description of the boy she remembered. Now the only word that came to mind was *hunk*. Her cheeks flamed, and she glanced down at the sketches in her hands to compose herself.

"What have you got there?" Noah patted Shorty on the shoulder and came toward her.

"Some ideas for new props."

He took them from her hands. "You didn't waste any time, did you?"

"There's no time to waste. Besides, I'm anxious to get started. I think this show can be one of the highlights of the weekend."

He held her gaze a moment as if reassessing her, then his clear blue eyes warmed, unleashing a sudden uneasiness. She pointed to the first sketch of a full-sized staircase: six steps with railings and a wide landing at the top. She shifted to his side to explain her idea and immediately regretted it. He smelled like he'd just stepped from the shower. The scent of soap and musky aftershave entwined around her senses, making her want to lean in close and inhale the tantalizing scent deep into her lungs.

"I thought a staircase would make that *Night Before Christmas* scene more homey and highlight the family Christmas theme. Stairs and fireplaces shout family, don't you think?" She looked up at him and her heart thumped. He was still staring at her. "Anyway, the tricky part is I want it to look like a staircase on this side, but on the other side I want it to be flat so it can be painted to look like a nativity backdrop for the next scene. That way we can simply turn it around, and we won't need two separate pieces."

"Clever. I like it."

"And it needs to be on wheels so we can move it around. Can you do that?"

"Sure. It'll take a little figuring, but it shouldn't be hard."

"Good. And about the Christmas tree. It's in all three acts, but it's too small. It needs to be twice that size and with more lights, and it has to be on a dolly so we can move it."

"The dolly I can help you with, but the tree is out of my area of expertise."

"I'll talk to Jen about that."

Noah shook his head, crossed his arms over his chest and looked down at her, making her aware of the muscle he'd acquired. His biceps and broad chest strained the fabric of the cotton shirt he wore. She looked up at him, thinking how the top of her head would nestle perfectly under his chin. She blinked and took a small step back, bracing for some sharp remark.

"I'm not sure bringing you on board was such a good idea." He leaned toward her. "I remember how you get. You charge forward like a little race car, dragging everyone behind you like tin cans on a string."

"I get excited."

"I know. It's what made being your friend so much fun." His smile grew tender, then abruptly vanished as if he was regretting the memory. "I have a feeling I'm going to be spending all my free time in the workshop."

She exhaled. "It'll keep you out of trouble."

His eyes suddenly darkened, and he pressed his lips together. "I think it's too late for that."

He walked off, calling out over his shoulder as he went. "I'll get right on this."

What did he mean about it being too late? Too late for them to repair their relationship? Spinning on her heel, she walked off. How was she supposed to make sense of anything with Noah when he hid behind that wall of resentment all the time? Every now and then he'd peek over the top and reminisce about their past. Then he'd duck down again.

Her mom's comments pushed into her mind, sending a feeling of shame along her nerves. In chasing her dream, she'd allowed all her relationships to fade away. It hadn't been a deliberate decision, but friendships hadn't seemed as important as becoming the best artist in the company. The one relationship she'd succumbed to had ended in disaster, and left her questioning every aspect of her life and career. She'd responded with even more determination and buried herself in her dancing, driving herself mercilessly. And now she was paying the price.

How did you balance the desires of your heart with the dedication to achieve your goal, and still find time to stay connected to those you loved? Was that even possible?

She could balance on the tips of her toes. She could pirouette and execute any number of precise moves with only the smallest part of her shoe touching the floor. But she'd never learned to balance her life.

With effort, she brushed the troublesome thought aside. She had new things to occupy her mind, and she liked it. Teaching the girls and working with the Christmas show provided a measure of satisfaction she hadn't experienced since her accident. That was a lot to be thankful for.

Sawdust flew around his head as Noah pushed the two-by-six through the table saw. The workshop behind his grandma's house had been his grandpa's domain. It's where Noah had learned to work with his hands. Gramps had been proud of his grandson's intellectual acumen, but he'd also wanted him to have a knowledge of basic handyman skills. Gramps had been a real estate developer by profession, but he'd been raised on a farm and worked his way through college as a carpenter. He'd headed the local Habitat for Humanity program in Dover and insisted Noah volunteer as often as possible. Noah had balked at first, preferring to have his nose in a book or a computer, but he soon realized that the special time with his gramps and helping people achieve a home of their own gave him a connection that meant more.

Noah switched off the saw and removed his safety glasses. The woodworking tools hadn't been touched in the two years since Gramps had passed, and it had taken Noah days to get them in order again. He'd resisted getting involved with the little theater when Gram had approached him. Being on the Board of Directors was one thing; getting involved with the actual production was something else. Now it had brought him even closer to Beth, which was the last thing he wanted. The harder he tried to keep his distance, the more they were thrust together.

"It's good to see this workshop in use again. Your granddad spent a lot of time in here. It was his therapy."

Noah grinned at his gram as she entered the shop. "I keep expecting him to look over my shoulder and point out my mistakes."

"He wanted you to do a good job." She stopped at his side. "What's this for?"

"Beth wants some new props built."

"I felt sure she'd bring new life to the show. Allison did her best, but she lacked vision. How is Beth getting along with everyone?"

Noah met her gaze. "Don't you mean how is she getting along with me?" His gram shrugged, a small smile on her lips.

"I always liked her."

"I did, too."

"Past tense?"

He sighed and slid on the safety glasses again. "She's doing a good job. Everyone likes her, and they like the changes she's adding. Your production is in good hands."

Gram patted his back. "Give her whatever she wants."

Noah sent another board through the saw, then shut it down again. What did Beth want? When he picked up Chloe from dance class, Beth was glowing with delight. At the theater, she vibrated with energy as she worked with the dancers. One thing he'd realized was that Beth's obsession came from her love of dancing. Yvonne's obsession sprang from an insatiable need to always be the center of attention. Yet in the back of his mind, he kept hearing her say she'd dance again—in New York. Not Dover.

Could she ever be content in a small town? He shook off the dangerous notion. No matter how strong his resolve to keep his heart protected from her, his heart had other ideas. The more time he spent with her, the more he thought about her. Their lives had become so intertwined that he had little chance to keep his distance.

Chloe had started to talk about Beth more than her mother. Another danger to avoid.

He stared at the wood he'd cut. All he could do for the moment was make Beth happy. The show had to succeed for Gram. Beth was something he'd have to deal with along the way.

Right now he had an appointment to inspect a house before he picked up Chloe at Beth's studio. Thank God for his inspector's job. It was the one time he could honestly say he didn't think about Beth. But the minute he stopped working, there she'd be again.

He *really* needed to get that under control before he ended up falling for her again.

Beth turned off the music and faced her students. "Good job today, ladies. I can't believe how quickly you're learning."

Hannah giggled. "That's 'cause it's so fun. I like you better than my other dance teacher."

Chloe nodded, a big smile on her face. "You're the best teacher ever."

Abby gave Chloe a friendly shove. "She's the only one you've had, silly."

The girls giggled as they gathered up their things. A horn honked, signaling that Julie had arrived to pick up Abby and Hannah, who lived next door to each other. "Remember, ladies, point those toes."

Abby and Hannah linked arms and chanted as they walked away. "Point your toes. Point your toes."

Chloe was standing at the barre trying to get her leg up on it, which made her look like a very awkward ballerina. The child was determined to learn, pushing for more and more new steps. Beth had to constantly remind her to be careful of her knee. "Chloe, why don't you practice your *demi pliés* while you wait. You might hurt yourself otherwise. I've already asked my brother to install the lower barre for you girls to use. It should be done by next lesson."

Chloe sighed and nodded, grasping the barre and placing her heels together.

Beth's cell chimed, and she hurried to pick it up from the back room. "Hey, Noah." Her heart fluttered at the sound of his voice.

"Could you take Chloe home for me today? I'm on a job site, and I won't be able to get away for another hour or so."

"I'd be happy to."

"Gram has a garden club meeting today and isn't answering her phone. I appreciate this. I'll make it up to you."

"No need. Friends help each other out."

There was a long pause before he responded. "Right. Thanks again."

Beth changed quickly into street clothes. Chloe talked nonstop on the way home. Evelyn's car wasn't in the drive when they arrived, so Beth went inside to stay with Chloe until she returned. She didn't have long to wait.

"What a nice surprise." Evelyn gave her a warm hug. "I was going to call you when I got home. I wanted to talk to you about something."

"The show?"

"No, something else. Let me fix you a glass of tea and we'll sit and talk."

Beth joined Evelyn in the small sunroom at the back of the house. "I've been telling my friends how you've helped Chloe, and we were wondering if dancing could help some of us with our arthritis and other issues. Phoebe—she lives next door and we've been friends since high school—mentioned some chair dancing that she'd read about online? She's in a wheelchair now, but she used to dance and she misses it."

Surprised at the request, Beth took a moment to consider it. "Dancing can be a huge benefit to older women. I'm sure I can do a little research and come up with something that would be fun for you."

"And my friends?"

"Of course, but my studio is small. There's barely room for me to work with the girls."

"Phoebe suggested we could meet at the senior center. There's plenty of room on the second floor, and we all spend time there off and on anyway."

"That's a good idea. I'll look into it and see what we could set up."

Evelyn smiled and patted her hand. "I can't tell you how glad I am that you came home to Dover. You have a lot to offer this town. I know you miss your career, but you could do so much here."

"Thank you. I'm still trying to figure out how to move forward without my dream, but I'm truly grateful for you getting me involved in the Christmas show. It feels good to be working again, even if it is on the other side of the stage." She rose and moved to the door, Evelyn close at her side.

"You know dear, the good Lord doesn't give us only one dream for our lives. He has a whole mountain of dreams and gifts He wants to give us. You simply have to hold out your hand to receive them."

She was starting to believe that. A few weeks ago she had despaired that nothing could fill the void left by her dancing. But now she woke up each morning looking forward to teaching others to dance. Was this the new dream the Lord was giving her? Or was she settling for what she could get?

A sudden desire raced through her to call Jen and talk things over the way they used to. It had been a long time since she'd had a real friend to share with. The women in the troupe were nice and she had made several friends, but the atmosphere was too competitive for really deep and lasting relationships. It was a part of her life that had become barren over the years, and she hadn't even noticed.

But even though she and Jen worked well together at the theater, and it felt as if they'd never been apart, she couldn't ignore the differences in their lives. Jen was a happily married working mother. How could she possibly understand the position Beth found herself in now? The thought brought tears to her eyes. Her past and her future were colliding in the present, and she didn't like it one bit.

Noah waited as Beth made her inspection of the moveable staircase he'd built. He'd painted and stained the steps and railing, but he'd leave the nativity backdrop in the hands of Eric Dobbs, the high school student who was the set designer and artist.

"Noah, it's perfect. Exactly like I imagined it. Thank you."

His shoulders eased with relief. He hadn't realized how much he wanted her to like his work. He wanted to please her. "Good. I'll start on the tree dolly next, but I wanted to finish this first since it took longer."

She smiled and lightly touched his arm, heating his skin and causing a miss in his heartbeat. He started to lay his hand over hers, but Jen joined them and he stepped back.

"This is awesome, Noah. It's going to make a huge statement in this number."

"It was all Beth's idea."

"I'm not surprised. This show is going to be so much better. You are a real blessing. I'm so glad you came home."

"I'm happy to help."

"Could I impose on you two to get us a bigger tree? Noah, I know you're building a dolly so we can move it, but that tree needs to be at least ten feet, don't you think?"

Beth nodded. "I'll take care of it."

Jen frowned. "Do you have a truck? An artificial tree that large, even boxed up, won't fit in a car."

"I don't, but my brothers do. I'll get one of them to take me shopping this weekend."

Jen shook her head. "Is there any way you could go sooner, like tonight or tomorrow? The clock is ticking, and we don't have much time to get these new changes in place."

"Why don't Beth and I go over to Sawyer's Bend tomorrow afternoon and pick one up?" Noah suggested. "I'm sure one of the big box stores will have a tree that size."

Noah studied Beth's expression. Apparently she wasn't too fond of the idea of going with him on the errand.

"You don't have to drive me. Linc and Gil both have trucks I can borrow."

Her hesitance spurred his amusement. "Nope. I'm the property guy, remember? But I need your artist's eye to pick out the right tree. Unless you don't want to go." He watched her internal debate reflected in her eyes and knew the moment she decided to accept.

"I do. Thanks for offering."

"Good. We can grab a bite to eat on the way." He felt like he'd just won a battle. For what, he didn't really know.

The soft look of longing in her eyes struck a chord. Did she long for the old camaraderie the way he did? He'd told himself to keep his distance, that renewing their old relationship could only end badly. But he found himself looking for ways to be close to her. Apparently he was incapable of learning some lessons.

"That would be nice. Like old times."

A cold rush of reality doused his good mood. Old times that had ended in heartbreak. The memory of when he realized she had cut him out of his life was like a thorn that never left his side. She would leave again. Maybe not today or next month, but she would, and he'd be left behind again. Only this time his child would be hurting, too.

"Not like old times. Those are over forever."

The look of hurt that flashed through her eyes tightened his throat, but he forced himself to walk away. He couldn't avoid Beth, but he sure could keep his protective shield in place.

Noah opened the door of his Silverado the next afternoon, placing his hand under Beth's elbow to steady her as she climbed into the large vehicle. As she settled into the cab, she suddenly realized that she was trapped in a small space with Noah. Not the ideal situation, given the tension between the two of them. She watched as he slid behind the wheel and fastened his seat belt. It was a good-sized cab, but cozy enough that she could catch a whiff of his aftershave and sense the warmth of his body. Yesterday this had seemed like a good idea, but now she realized she should never have agreed to this excursion.

Noah started the engine then glanced over at her. "I checked online, and it looks like Cost Saver Market should have a ten-foot tree. We'll stop there first."

"I appreciate you doing this."

He grinned, his blue eyes filled with a friendly glint. "I like shopping for Christmas trees. It's my favorite time of year. I'd prefer a live tree, but that wouldn't work for the show."

"No." At a loss for topics to discuss, she clasped her hands in her lap, listening to the strains of "Hark! The Herald Angels Sing" coming from the truck's radio.

"You're doing a great job on the show. And it looks to me like you're having a good time."

"I am. It's more fun than I expected." Another lull in the conversation lasted for nearly a mile. They used to never lack things to talk about. Now, every subject threatened to open up an old wound or a door better left closed. She started when Noah suddenly spoke up.

"Can I ask you something? What did you mean the other day when you said you didn't think I'd care if you left town?"

She stared out the window. This was not what she wanted to discuss, especially trapped in a vehicle with no way to escape. Then again, maybe it was time to face the past and clear the air. "Because that's how I felt."

"Why would you think that?"

The memory of that day and the humiliation burned inside. How could she explain that he'd broken her heart without admitting she'd been in love with him? "You made your feelings very clear when I came by your house that afternoon. I knew you were embarrassed by my gift. You tried to let me down easy, but I was so humiliated I just wanted to run back home."

"What are you talking about?"

She sighed and closed her eyes briefly, fighting the old pain that was reforming inside. "The graduation gift I gave you that afternoon."

"You mean that key ring with the odd shape?"

He hadn't even noticed the symbolic nature of her present. He was rubbing salt into her open wounds. "It was a stylized heart. I had it engraved on the back."

"You did? I don't remember seeing that."

Beth jerked her head to look at him. Was that possible? Had he not read the words that had taken her hours to compose, words that revealed her deepest emotion? "Then why did you act so nervous and uncomfortable?"

"Because I didn't have your gift ready. We weren't supposed to exchange them until that night in the gazebo. I hadn't wrapped your present and I was still working on my speech. You threw me a curve when you showed up without warning in the middle of the day. Wait. You had that thing engraved? What did it say?"

Beth bit the inside of her mouth. She couldn't tell him now. It would put them both in an uncomfortable position. She tried to choose her words carefully. "It was just a BFF kind of sentiment. You were leaving for Mississippi State the next morning, and we wouldn't see each other much over the summer. I wanted to make sure you didn't forget me. Our friendship was very important to me. But after your reaction, I thought you were anxious to leave Dover. And me."

He glanced over at her, his brow furrowed, his blue eyes clouded. "No. Never. I cared about you very much. I was worried we'd drift apart, too, so I was writing a speech to give you along with your gift. I just never got the chance. You were gone the next morning, and I had to no idea where or why. When I found out you'd joined the Forsythe Company and never bothered to tell me, I figured…" He stared straight ahead, his jaw flexing. "It doesn't matter what I figured."

Beth studied his profile, outlined by the truck window. He'd never read her heartfelt message, and she'd misinterpreted his reaction to her gift. They'd cleared the air, but nothing had really changed. She'd still left without telling him and shut him out of her life. He would never know she'd offered him her heart, and he'd never said he cared for her beyond friendship. The damage had been done.

What now? Could they rebuild their relationship? Could he accept it was all a misunderstanding and forgive her? She'd hurt him deeply, and she couldn't go back and fix that mistake. And it wasn't just her abandonment that he'd endured. Yvonne had further dismantled his belief in women and in love. All he'd ever wanted was a family, and his dream had been shattered.

"I'm sorry, Noah. I waited too long. I didn't mean to cut you out of my life." She held her breath, hoping for some words of encouragement, a peace offering.

"We can't go back and change the past. But we can learn from it."

What did he mean? "Can we call a truce? For the good of the show." She watched a muscle in his jaw flex.

"Sure. Why not? For the good of the show."

Any hope she might have had for their relationship floated off like a feather in the wind. His cold, flat tone of voice spoke far more than his words.

Beth pressed closer to the glass in the front window of the real estate office, straining to see all the activity taking place around town. Trucks with elevated buckets and platforms carried men who were attaching lights to the facades of every old building. Others were hanging Christmas drapes across the streets while a crew scurried around the courthouse square setting up the traditional nativity and other lighted shapes. The entire downtown was filled with workers. "I had no idea there would be so many lights put up around town."

"There are twice as many this year. I get giddy just thinking about it. I know you weren't here long enough to see what Gemma accomplished last Christmas, but I think in a few years Dover might become one of the must-see holiday attractions in the state."

"I have to admit, we're both looking forward to the big lighting ceremony."

"We?"

Beth cringed. She'd have to watch her tongue around her mother. She gave a nonchalant shrug. "Noah and I were talking about it on the way home from buying the tree yesterday. The streets were blocked off so we had to take the back way to the theater."

"How nice. Maybe you can watch the grand lighting together. It's really quite spectacular."

Time to change the subject. "Do you know where Tori keeps her holiday decorations? I think I'll put up a tree this year and maybe string some lights along the balcony."

"There's storage space in the back of the guest bedroom closet, but you'll need help getting it out. Maybe Noah can help you."

Absolutely not. "I'm perfectly capable of getting stuff out of a closet."

"Normally I would agree. However, some of the boxes are heavy, and you don't need to be putting extra stress on your knee. It wouldn't hurt to have a pair of strong arms around."

No, it wouldn't hurt, but those arms wouldn't belong to Noah. They'd been getting along nicely since their truce had been declared, but while he'd lowered his wall, it was still far too high for her to climb over.

"I think we should go all out for the storefront-window decorating contest this year, too. I did the bare minimum last year, and Noah's office was vacant. Maybe you and Noah could come up with something to coordinate both windows."

Beth rolled her eyes. "Mom. Don't try to play matchmaker. I'm not looking for any kind of relationship, and I'm sure Noah isn't, either. Especially with me." She muttered that last part under her breath.

"Well, I don't know why not. You two were thick as thieves in high school. Besides, he's a very attractive man, in case you missed that. Evelyn swears women stop in their tracks and stare at him when he walks by. But he never even notices."

Beth had no doubt about that. With his broad shoulders, touchable, wavy dark hair and those blue eyes that could melt your insides with one glance, he was the ultimate masculine package. The icing on the cake was that he had no idea he was handsome. She felt sure that in his mind, he was still that skinny, geeky kid no one paid any attention to. It was a trait that made him all the more appealing.

Beth shook her head to dislodge the thought, but her gaze drifted to the office window next door. She stopped and caught her breath. Chloe had her arms wrapped around Noah, her head pressed against his chest as he patted her back. Beth moved to the door to get a closer look.

"Mom. Something's wrong." Without a second thought, she hurried over to Noah's office.

"Chloe, are you okay?" She touched the child's shoulder, her gaze locking with Noah's. His eyes darkened as he shook his head, and a muscle in his jaw flexed rapidly.

Chloe shifted her head against her dad's chest and looked at Beth with tearful, sad eyes. "I didn't get a ticket, and tomorrow is Thanksgiving."

Beth's heart sank. Her mother had let her down. "Oh, Chloe, I'm so sorry."

"Is everything all right?"

Beth glanced over her shoulder as her mother joined them, but before she could explain, Chloe broke from Noah's arms and plunged into Francie's.

"I can't spend Thanksgiving with my mom."

"Oh, sweetie. I'm so sorry."

"I was going to meet Dustin Baker and all kinds of famous people. Now it'll be an old boring day with just Dad and Gram."

Noah's mouth pinched, and his brow furrowed. Her heart went out to him. She felt certain he knew Chloe didn't mean what she said, but it probably stung at any rate. How could a dad and grandmother compete with the rich and famous in Hollywood? But maybe she could soften the blow a little bit.

She caught her mother's gaze. "How about Thanksgiving dinner with a not quite as famous ballerina and her family?"

Her mother's face brightened with delight at the suggestion. "That's a wonderful idea. Why don't you and your dad and grandma come and spend the day with us? You already know Abby and Evan. We play football in the afternoon, and we have the dogs running around and all kinds of fun things to do." She stroked Chloe's hair and looked at Noah. "Please. We'd love to have your family join us. We have plenty of room and more than enough food."

Noah considered the idea. "That's very kind of you, but I think Gram already has some food prepared."

"Just bring it with you." She set Chloe away from her and smiled. "Will you come, Chloe?"

She wiped tears from her cheeks and looked over at her father. "Can we? Please?"

Beth grinned at the resigned look on Noah's face. She knew he probably didn't want to spend the holiday with her, but it's not like they'd be alone or anything. They'd barely have time to talk.

"I'll have to check with your grandma, Chloe."

Francie waved off his concerns. "Leave that to me. I'll give Evelyn a call right now and arrange everything. Thanksgiving is more fun with lots of family. Since you're my renter, that qualifies you. Besides, we'll be a couple members short this year. Tori is still in California, and Seth is a newly minted Houston police officer, so he's working."

Francie took Chloe's hand and went back to the office, leaving Beth with Noah. He was worrying his bottom lip with his finger as if rethinking the idea.

"I'm sorry her plans didn't work out."

"I knew they wouldn't, and I tried to prepare her, but she won't listen. Once she gets an idea in her head it's hard to get it out."

"Family trait, huh?"

"Yeah. I guess."

"I hope I didn't make this awkward for you with my invitation. Mom's right, though. We're used to having a full house for the holiday, and we're short this year. You'll be our fill-ins."

"A fill-in family. Should I be honored or insulted?"

She tilted her head. "That's up to you. I just wanted to cheer Chloe up. She had her heart set on going to see her mom."

"We don't always get what we set our hearts on. You should know that better than anyone." He paused and took a deep breath. "I didn't mean to sound judgmental. It never gets any easier."

"This happens a lot?"

"Too many times to count."

She reached out and touched his arm. "I'm sorry. For both of you." His blue eyes softened with affection, sending a sweet warmth curling through her rib cage. It was the look she'd seen in his eyes frequently those last few months before they'd graduated. The one that had convinced her he was secretly in love with her the way she was with him. "I'd better get back. Is it okay for Chloe to stay with us for a while longer?"

"Sure. I'll finish up here and then come get her."

At the door to the real estate office, Beth looked

back to see Noah rubbing his forehead before placing his palms on the desk and bowing his head. How many times had he been forced to endure his child's disappointment? She'd known a lot of disappointment in her life and it had been deeply painful, but experiencing Chloe's had hurt in a way she'd never known before. What must it feel like to be a father?

On the heels of that thought came one from her own conscience. How many times had her family been disappointed when she canceled a trip home or failed to remember a birthday?

She couldn't go back and fix the past, but she knew she didn't want to be that out of touch with the people she loved ever again. Seeing the sadness in Chloe's eyes held up a mirror to her own failures.

And she didn't like the picture it revealed.

Chapter Six

Noah had never experienced a Thanksgiving dinner like this one. He'd agreed to spending the holiday with the Montgomerys in a moment of weakness and had been regretting his decision ever since. Even reminding himself it was for Chloe's sake hadn't helped ease his anxiety.

His grandparents had always celebrated with quiet formality, in a solemn and dignified fashion. He'd expected the Montgomerys to be the same. He'd anticipated being on edge and feeling awkward in the midst of a family gathering with no connection to his familiar traditions. But Beth's family was boisterous and fun-loving. While the table was set with fine china, silver and crystal, the atmosphere was relaxed and casual, and it was obvious they enjoyed being together.

It reminded him of holidays growing up with his parents. Being surrounded by this large family renewed his hopes that he could give his daughter a complete family one day.

He took another bite of the melt-in-your-mouth cornbread dressing Beth had prepared and tried not to moan with delight. He had no idea Beth could cook, even though her mother had touted her skills before the Thanksgiving dinner.

He glanced around the table at the Montgomerys assembled for the holiday meal. Gram was seated next to Francie, and the two women giggled and chatted between bites like teenagers. They had been friends for a long time, but after they'd each lost a spouse, they had a deeper bond now.

Beth's brothers were clearly crazy in love with their new wives. Her sisters-in-law were beautiful women— Gemma a stunning strawberry blonde with sparkling eyes, and Julie a lovely brunette with a megawatt smile. But neither could hold a candle to Bethany's serene, elegant beauty. Maybe it was her years of dance training that gave her the graceful carriage, or maybe she'd been born with it and that's what had made her such an exceptional ballerina. Either way, she was the most fascinating woman he'd ever met, a unique combination of femininity and strength.

He glanced at Beth. How had she lived in New York away from this kind of support for so long? She'd always claimed that she didn't fit in here, but she looked relaxed and happy to him. She caught him looking at her and smiled, making his mouth suddenly dry and his palms sweaty. He hated the way his body reacted whenever she looked at him or touched him. He'd strengthened his defenses today, but when she'd opened the door to the Montgomery home with her welcoming smile, they'd tilted like the Leaning Tower of Pisa. The dark slacks she wore emphasized her long legs, and the soft teal top with the scooped neck showed off the graceful curve of her shoulders. Earrings with

tiny stars bobbed around her chin, adding even more
sparkle to her pretty eyes.

All in all, he was glad he'd agreed to come today.
As close as he and Beth had been, he'd never spent
any time with her family. Her older brothers had been
away at college or working for the family business.
But he'd been welcomed today with handshakes and
smiles. They'd inquired about his new business, and
offered to pass his name along to the architects they
knew. They said they would do whatever they could
to help him get established.

A giggle drew his attention to his daughter. Mostly
he was glad he'd come because of the smile that was
now back on Chloe's face after a long night of tears.
She and Abby were seated together talking nonstop,
waving forks in the air to punctuate their conversation. He marveled at the resiliency of his child. Time
after time, her mother let her down, broke promises
and failed to follow through on plans. Chloe would
cry, but then get back up, convinced that one day her
mom would come through. She shamed him with her
faith and loyalty. Unfortunately, he knew that loyalty
had its limits.

His gaze drifted immediately to Beth. Where were
her loyalties? With her career, or with her family?

The tapping of metal on glass drew everyone's attention. Gil stood. "Before we have our dessert, we
have an announcement to make."

Abby jumped up. "Can I tell? Please? I've waited
forever."

Gil chuckled and reached down to take his wife's
hand. "Go ahead, sweet pea."

Abby clapped her hands and bounced up and down. "I'm going to be a big sister."

The room erupted with cheers and laughter, and questions were flung at the couple. Beside him, Beth remained silent. Her smile was forced, and her hands gripped her napkin tightly. He watched as she closed her eyes briefly. When she opened them, her attitude had changed. She stood.

"Now we're really ready for dessert. Let's celebrate with Mom's pecan pie."

Noah glanced around the room. Everyone was pre-occupied and didn't seem to notice the strain in Beth's voice. He rose and picked up his plate, following her to the kitchen.

He found her standing at the counter, pie cutter in hand but not moving. Her shoulders were slumped as if she was too weary to proceed. He stopped at her side, fighting the urge to pull her into a hug to comfort her. "Are you all right?"

The sadness in her eyes when she looked at him pierced every nerve ending.

"What's wrong?"

"Nothing. I'm fine."

"I know you're not. Talk to me."

"I think you might have been right. I did pay too high a price for my career." The mellow tones of classical music intruded. She pulled her phone from the small pocket on her top and looked at the screen.

"I have to take this." Turning her back, she disappeared from the kitchen.

When the pie had been served and she hadn't reappeared, Noah went looking for her. Gil directed him to the office off the foyer. She was curled up in one of the leather chairs, legs tucked beneath her, staring out the window. Her cell phone was still clutched in her hand. "Beth."

She glanced up and saw him, and the worry in her eyes pricked his throat. Something was wrong. He considered leaving her alone. If she needed his help, she could ask for it. But he couldn't leave her alone like this. Slowly he moved toward her, taking a seat in the chair next to her. When she didn't withdraw, he braved a question. "Bad news?"

"Maybe. Probably." She chewed her bottom lip and clutched the phone to her chest. "A friend called from the ballet company. There's a rumor that a new artistic director is coming in, and she's going to void all our contracts and renegotiate."

"Can she do that?"

"It's happened before. My contract is up in February. I was hoping to be back by then, but I won't be ready to perform again for several more months, if then."

"You're their star. Surely they wouldn't let you go. Don't you have an agent or someone that can handle this for you?"

She shook her head. "Most ballet dancers don't have agents. And I'm an injured star who hasn't danced for nine months. The rumor is Noreen Andrews is taking over, and she's never been one of my fans."

He wanted to reach out his hand, but she was so closed off, he doubted she'd accept his sympathy. He searched for something comforting to say. "You should check with your attorney. Maybe you should resign and cut your losses."

She nodded, wiping a tear from her eyes. "But if I

do that, it means it's truly over. I'm done. I'm not ready to accept that."

Noah set his jaw. Now he knew where her loyalties were. She was still focused on getting back to her other life. "Do you really think you can get back to the level you were once at? Honestly?"

"Yes. Other dancers have overcome this type of injury. I can, too."

Small shards of ice cut across his insides. He stood. "Well, knowing how obsessed you are, I'm sure you'll be back onstage in no time."

He pivoted and walked back into the family room, where Linc and Gil promptly drew him into a game of football on the front lawn. He welcomed the diversion. Physical exertion was exactly what he needed to work off that big dinner.

But he knew he was lying to himself. He needed to work off his anger and disappointment in Beth. She would never, *ever* change.

With the real estate office closed the day after Thanksgiving, Beth used the time to begin decorating the windows for the upcoming contest. She'd been dragging her feet on this project, mainly because her mother had wanted her to do Noah's window, too, so they'd match. After yesterday, she doubted Noah would welcome her invading his office to put up Christmas decorations. Each time she thought they'd made progress toward restoring their old friendship, something would drive them apart again. Usually it involved her career.

Thanksgiving with the Carlisles had gone well, though not as she'd expected. She'd counted on her large family to act as a buffer between her and Noah, but his presence had instead been an electrified magnet, drawing her attention to his every movement. He seemed to enjoy all the hustle and bustle, but there'd been times when he'd looked a bit overwhelmed, even melancholy. When they'd taken their places at the table, the tension between them had intensified. They'd ended up on one corner of the long table, making it impossible to avoid eye contact or bumping knees. After the third apology, she'd given up.

During the blessing, Beth had taken Noah's hand, his touch sending little jolts of awareness up her arm and swirling around her heart. When the prayer ended, he'd clung to her fingers a long moment before letting go. She looked into his eyes, searching for an explanation, but he only smiled and looked away, giving her hope that he might be ready to forgive her.

Then the phone call about her contract had come, and now she was on his bad side again. He'd tried to comfort her and she'd raised her defenses, declaring she would dance again and pushing him away. She'd taken his advice, however, and made an appointment to talk to the family attorney, Blake Prescott, to go over her contract.

Hopefully, working on the window would keep her mind off her troubles. Locating her sister's stash of Christmas decorations was easy. Getting them out of the narrow crawl space behind the closet was something else. Nothing was heavy, just awkward, and she was concerned about twisting her knee. She made a mental note to call one of her brothers to get the boxes out. She'd managed to retrieve one container filled with craft ribbons and other items, and she maneuvered it down to the office.

The old building's display window consisted of a raised platform, a common feature in the past as a means to showcase merchandize. It was a charming touch, but it made it awkward at times to hang posters and other things. She used to worry that her mother would forget about the twelve-inch rise and would lose her balance. Now that worry was for her own safety.

Opening the lid, she rummaged through the carton, silently thanking her sister for being so organized. Every item was neatly packaged and labeled. However, now it was up to her to create some kind of holiday design out of the bits and pieces. She'd never been as good at that as Tori. There was an abundance of white paper and red ribbon. She fingered the items, trying to jump-start the long-dormant creative part of her brain. The white paper reminded her of the church steeple of Peace Community rising above the trees. A memory surfaced of her and Tori making piles of paper snowflakes and trees to hang around the house. The thought made her smile. It might actually be relaxing to sit and cut out paper shapes.

After pulling up her playlist of Christmas music, she selected an album then settled in, folding and cutting various designs, large and small. Her mother had told her there was a small white artificial tree in the back storage room of the office. The more she worked, the more her ideas grew. And so did her satisfaction. The window might not win an award in the contest, but it would be attractive.

She was securing the last red ribbon to the corner of the window when someone tapped on the glass. Chloe smiled and waved. She waved back and went outside to join her. Noah was there, causing her to come up short. For some reason, she'd expected Chloe to be with Evelyn.

He looked ruggedly handsome today in a plaid button-up shirt in soft colors, faded jeans and a sleeveless zip-up vest that made his shoulders appear impossibly broad. She couldn't tell from the closed expression on his face if he was still irked with her, so she turned her attention to the little girl. "What do you think?"

"I love it."

"I still have to decorate the tree and add lights." She stepped back and examined the arrangement. Overall she was pleased. It could use a touch of greenery and maybe a contrasting color, too. Something to make it all pop, but she'd tackle that later.

"Where did you get the big snowflakes, Miss Beth?"

"I made them."

Her eyes widened. "Can you teach me?"

Beth laid her arm across the child's shoulders. "Of course. It's easy."

"And can we do our window the same so we'll match?"

Noah stepped forward. "Chloe, I'm sure Miss Beth doesn't have time to do our window, too."

A bubble of perverse glee caused her to smile. It was nice to shove the rigid Noah off his foundation sometimes. "Actually, my mother has asked me to do both windows, so it's not a problem."

"Can I help? I like decorating."

"Of course." She ignored the deep frown that had formed on Noah's brow. "We can do it now if it's all right with your father."

Chloe nodded enthusiastically. "Is it okay, Daddy?"

"Do I have a choice?"

She and Chloe glanced at each other before turning to face him. "No."

Their simultaneous response sealed the deal. They shared a smile, linked arms and went back inside the office.

Beth eased her conscience by remembering Noah's declaration that he couldn't say no to his child. This time it had worked to her advantage.

Noah leaned back in his office chair, pinching the bridge of his nose. He'd decided to work while Beth and Chloe decorated the front office window. With several reports due and calculations to make on a few structural situations, he had plenty to keep him busy. His new plotter, the large printer he used for blueprints, had been delivered and needed to be set up.

The office was quiet at the moment. Beth had taken Chloe to the store to pick up more decorations for the window. They'd run out of paper and red ribbon. He'd welcomed their departure to focus on his work, but found the office strangely lonely with them gone.

He'd chosen to work here in the back office as they went about their business, but it had been hard to concentrate. The wide opening in the wall between the spaces made it easy to see and hear customers as they entered. But it had the opposite effect when two females were decorating a Christmas window. They'd worked quietly, but the soft giggles and happy chatter had distracted him. After the huge disappointment Chloe had suffered thanks to her mother, he was glad the holiday weekend was providing some enjoyment for her. He just wasn't sure how he felt about Beth being the source.

Watching them work together had unleashed a flood of warmth and longing deep inside of Noah. Chloe was missing out on having a woman in her life. Gram was great, but the age difference sometimes became an issue. Beth was young, enthusiastic and close in age to Chloe's mom. Though Yvonne had always been more concerned with her own enjoyment than her child's. There were times when he seriously considered marrying again to give his daughter a mother. But he couldn't get beyond the knowledge that he'd failed twice.

Rising, he walked into the front office and stopped. The room had been hit by a craft tornado. Tiny slivers of white paper littered the desk and floor like confetti. Ribbon in various lengths curled on every surface. Instead of being irked, he chuckled at the mess. Chloe was having fun. That's all that mattered.

Suddenly the pair entered like a burst of energy, laughing and cradling bundles of items for the window. He frowned at the large assortment. "I don't think there's room in that one window for all this stuff."

"Some of it's for Beth's apartment, Daddy. She can't reach the boxes in the closet so she bought some new things."

He looked to Beth for an explanation.

"My sister has all her Christmas decorations shoved in the back of her closet, and they're too heavy for me to pull out." She gestured toward her knee. "Normally it wouldn't be a problem, but I don't want to risk it right now."

"I'll pull it out for you. You should have just asked." What was he saying? When had he become her rescuer?

"Oh, that's all right. I'll get one of the boys to come by."

"Don't be silly. I'm right here. Besides, it's the least I can do to thank you for decorating the window." She smiled, and his heart dipped into his stomach.

"Thanks. We'll do that as soon as we're finished here."

Working was pointless. He gave up and offered himself as the token tall person to fetch the things too high for them to reach. When the window was done, there remained an empty spot that begged for a tree.

"Is this where our tree will go? Do I need to go buy one?"

Beth set her hands on her hips, her mouth puckered into a thoughtful—and adorable—grimace. "Not sure yet. A white tree to match the one in our window would be the obvious solution, but I'd like to see what else I can find."

"So are you done?" He studied the window. White paper snowflakes bobbed in the air along with red streamers. They'd cut out shapes to look like snowdrifts and taped them to the bottom and edges of the window like a frame. He would never have thought of using simple paper and ribbons to decorate.

"For now."

Chloe nodded. "We need an accent color. We've decided that it should be aqua."

Noah had no idea what they were talking about. Aqua? That wasn't a Christmas color.

Chloe reached into one of the larger sacks and pulled out a figure of a peacock in hues of aqua. "This is for Miss Beth's window, and she's still looking for one for ours."

"Maybe my sister has something in her closet."

"Now's as good a time as any to find out." There he went again, volunteering his help when there was no need. Beth looked as surprised as he felt.

"Thanks. Give me a few minutes to put this stuff away and straighten up the office."

Noah watched her go, suddenly aware that she'd taken a considerable amount of energy with her when she left. His office didn't seem nearly as bright and cheerful without her.

"Daddy, I love Miss Beth. Isn't she wonderful?"

She was something. He just hadn't decided what yet. He cleared his throat, which was unusually tight. "She's a very nice lady." Beautiful, strong, compassionate— and determined to leave Dover. "Let's clean this up."

A half hour later, Noah pulled the last box from the crawl space in Beth's closet and stood. There was no way, with her injury, she could have done this on her own. He was glad he'd been here to help. He placed the plastic container near the others in the living room.

Chloe dashed in from the balcony. She'd been watching the vendors arriving in the square for the grand lighting kickoff this evening. "Wow, that's a lot of boxes. Can we open them now?"

Noah picked up her jacket and tossed it to her. "It's time to go. I'm sure Miss Beth would like some time to sort through these things on her own."

Chloe slipped on her jacket, glancing over her shoulder at the balcony. "Are you going to watch all the lights come on tonight?"

"Of course. I'm looking forward to it. I think it's going to be spectacular."

Chloe bit her lip, an impish smile lifting the corner

of her mouth. "I think your balcony would be the best place to watch from."

"Chloe." Now his daughter was playing matchmaker, too. Or was she simply looking for more time with Beth and a perfect vantage point to see the lights? Either scenario was not good.

Beth must have read his reluctance because she slipped an arm across Chloe's shoulders and gave him a challenging smile. "I think you're right. Why don't you come back this evening? I'll fix supper, and we can watch the lights come on together. Wouldn't that be fun?"

No. No way. He was spending too much time with Beth as it was.

"Please, Daddy. That would be so totally cool."

He sighed. He had a sturdy spine and it worked to perfection, except when his little girl made those puppy dog eyes, and her voice went up three levels, and she asked him for something she really wanted. Then those healthy vertebrae turned to jelly. Gram was going out to dinner with friends this evening, so he'd been looking at ordering pizza. If Beth's cornbread stuffing was any gauge, she would probably serve a tastier meal than he'd been planning.

"Fine. What can I bring?"

"Nothing but yourselves."

They started for the door, but Chloe stopped and spun around. "Do you need any help with supper? I help Gram all the time."

Noah froze. "Chloe, it's not nice to invite yourself to people's homes."

"I'm not. I'm offering to help. That's different."

Not in his view, but when he saw the grin on Beth's face, he knew he was licked.

"Chloe, you are just full of good ideas today. I'd love to have your help. In fact, it's nearly time to start preparing anyway. You could stay, and your dad could supervise."

Talk about being ganged up on. How was a guy supposed to stay strong when he had two beautiful women working against him? "You can stay, but I'm going back to the office to work. That window-decorating session cost me some time."

Beth helped Chloe remove her jacket. "Fine. You do that, and we'll call you when everything is ready."

Noah opened the door and headed down the stairs. As he entered his office, he felt the silence in a way he hadn't before. Worse still, he was looking forward to the meal and to watching the lights go on all over downtown. He wanted to see that childlike sparkle in Beth's eyes. The thought of seeing his daughter and his friend experience the grand lighting filled him with joyful anticipation. He sent a quick text to his gram explaining the change in plans, knowing she would be smiling happily at the turn of events.

As he stepped into his office, the delicate snowflakes and ribbons in the window fluttered, reminding him of the video he'd watched last night of Beth. Red reminded him of her strength and determination. White conjured up all her feminine traits. How could the thing he admired most about her be the thing that kept them apart?

He owed Beth a debt of gratitude for helping to lift Chloe's spirits and forget about her mom's broken promise. But he worried he was trading one bad situation for another. Beth still had every intention of returning to dancing, which meant the heartbreak would be deeper when the dance world lured her back.

He was standing in a bed of wet cement, and it was hardening around him faster than he could pull himself out.

The bell on his office door chimed, and he looked up to see a slender middle-aged man enter. "Can I help you?"

The man gave him a quick once-over with piercing dark eyes. "You the engineer?"

"Yes, sir. Noah Carlisle." He extended his hand. "What can I do for you?"

"Harvey Kramer. I'm remodeling a house out on Old Agler Road, and I need an engineer to check things out to make sure the changes I want to make are possible."

"I can help you with that. Have a seat and tell me what you're looking at doing."

Noah sent up a grateful prayer. Nothing better to take his mind off Beth and Chloe than his first client. This was something he understood and could control.

Chapter Seven

Beth slid the casserole dish into the oven and closed the door, double-checking the temperature before setting the timer. Anticipation over the meal with Chloe and Noah bubbled up, making her feel lighter than she had in a long while. She loved to cook, but with little free time and no one to cook for, she'd rarely taken the time.

Making one small adjustment to the fall-themed place mat she'd put at Noah's place, she scolded herself for being so particular. He'd never notice the table decorations. Not the way she'd noticed him as he'd wrestled the boxes from the tight storage space. Every masculine movement had captivated her attention. The muscles in his arms and back had flexed appealingly as he'd tugged the boxes from the deep space. His jeans had stretched tightly over his thighs as he stooped to place them on the floor. He'd caught her staring more than once, but she dismissed her interest as the need to make sure he didn't miss any boxes or break anything fragile.

The truth was, she liked watching Noah. She liked

the little groan in his throat as he hoisted a heavy box. She liked the way he had to repeatedly brush his wavy hair from his forehead. She liked many things about him. But she shouldn't.

Chloe came in from the balcony for the tenth time, her impatience growing. "There sure are a lot of people down there. When did you say the lights will go on?"

"Seven o'clock. You still have an hour to wait."

They'd worked together, making the chicken-and-mushroom casserole and preparing fresh rolls. Chloe proved to be an entertaining and helpful assistant. Now they had to wait forty-five minutes before they could eat.

"Can we look in the boxes now?"

"Sure. In fact, let's start with this big one because I'm hoping there's a garland I can drape over the balcony railing." As expected, a large garland was coiled neatly in the bottom. Bright gold bulbs were intertwined among the long faux evergreen strand and accented with lights and strings of beads. It would look lovely draped along her balcony rail. The next box they opened held tabletop decorations her sister had collected.

Chloe hummed along with "Frosty the Snowman" playing in the background before pulling out a sturdy snow globe with a white church in the center. She shook it to set the flakes in motion. "I love Christmas. It's so pretty and happy. I think it would be fun to spend each Christmas in a different place so I could see how other people decorate."

"That would be fun, but if you're away for the holiday, you won't be with your family."

"I'd take them with me. It's only Gram and Daddy."

Beth chuckled softly as she tried to envision wrangling all her family members in one direction. But they'd never leave the family home at the holidays. A sharp stab of regret pricked her heart when she thought about the many Christmases she'd missed and could never recapture. This Christmas would be one she would cherish because it would be one she fully embraced. "I couldn't do that. There are too many of us."

Chloe nodded. "I wish my mom would come home for Christmas." She shook the globe again, watching the mini snowstorm.

Her melancholy tone pinched Beth's conscience. Chloe's disappointment from the last holiday was still so fresh. "I'm sorry you weren't able to go to see her over Thanksgiving."

Chloe offered a small smile and a shrug. "She's very busy and very important. That's why she forgets about me sometimes." She shifted and looked Beth in the eye, her smile confident. "But she loves me. I know when she sees me again, she'll remember how much she misses me, and then we'll spend more time together and go places and have adventures."

Beth forced a smile. From what she'd learned from Noah, Chloe's hopes would likely never be realized. She wanted to hug the little girl close and try to explain the behavior of adults, but she had a feeling Chloe's belief was too strong to be swayed by truth. Eventually she'd have to come to terms with her mother's indifference. She prayed Noah would handle that time carefully.

Noah arrived just as the timer dinged on the casserole. They worked together to get the food on the table, and Noah gave the blessing.

Beth was thankful that Chloe's excited chatter prevented any conversation between her and Noah. She liked looking across the table and seeing Noah there. Mostly she liked the feeling of inclusion that being together created. It wasn't too different from the feeling she had when she performed. If someone had told her she could have that feeling outside *pointe* shoes, she would have scoffed. But here she was, in her sister's apartment with an attractive man and his adorable daughter, feeling more like she belonged than she had in a long time.

"Beth."

She blinked and looked at Noah. "What?"

He grinned. "You wandered off for a moment. I was complimenting you on your casserole. I never knew you were such a good cook."

"Thank you."

Chloe twisted in her chair and looked out the front window. "Is it time yet?"

Noah checked his watch. "Almost."

"Why don't you two go out on the balcony while I clean up? By then it should be close to seven."

Noah stood but he didn't follow his daughter outside. He picked up his plate and carried it to the sink.

"You don't have to do that."

"Oh, yes, I do. If my gram found out I didn't help clear the table, I'd be in the doghouse for a week."

"Well, I'd hate to see you forced to endure that horrible fate."

He laughed, causing her to study him a moment. "You're in a good mood."

"I am. While you were preparing the meal, I was landing my first private client. He's restoring an old house out on Old Agler Road, and he needs an engineer to go over the place."

"That's wonderful. Congratulations."

"Thanks. It's a small start. Hopefully once I get connected with a few local architects, I'll get into the commercial business deals. That's what I really enjoy."

Beth glanced at the clock. "Oh. It's almost time." The temperature had dropped, and the lightweight sweater she wore wouldn't provide much warmth. She lifted a throw from the sofa as she headed for the balcony, but Noah took it from her, opened it and gently draped it around her shoulders. His arm lingered awhile, making her aware of the warmth of him and the nearness.

He looked into her eyes as if searching for something. His arm urged her forward.

"Beth."

Her name was a whisper, soft and caressing. She knew what he was asking, and she raised her head in response.

"Daddy, look at all the people. And there's the carriage going by."

They pulled apart and joined Chloe on the balcony as she leaned over the rail, watching the crowds of visitors milling around in anticipation of the grand lighting event.

Beth allowed her gaze to scan the square, chasing the moment with Noah to the back of her mind. "Mom told me this was a big deal, but I had no idea. I can't remember ever seeing so many people in our little town."

"I hope it's worth it."

She opened her mouth to scold Noah for his negative comment, but saw the twinkle in his blue eyes and gave him a playful punch in the shoulder instead.

Suddenly, the streetlamps, storefronts and other usual lights in the square blinked out. The crowd hushed in anticipation. Then in an instant, the lights flashed on in a dazzling display of color, illuminating the entire square. The courthouse glowed with tiny lights from the dome to the pillars on each side. The historic gazebo was awash in white lights. Large standing displays in different colors dotted the park. Every storefront, from sidewalk to roof parapet, was ablaze with twinkling Christmas lights. The oohs and aahs went on for several minutes before changing to loud applause and shouts of approval. From speakers above the crowds, Christmas carols filled the air.

Beth wiped tears of delight from her eyes.

Chloe exhaled a soft sigh. "Daddy, it's the most beautiful thing I've ever seen."

"I'd have to agree."

"I didn't expect it to be this spectacular and moving. Gemma told me she wanted the lights to reflect the glory of God's arrival here on earth. I think she succeeded."

They watched in silence for a few moments, gazing in wonder and appreciation at the glory of it all. Noah placed his arms on the railing, bringing his shoulder into contact with hers, making her acutely aware of his warmth and the heady scent of his aftershave.

"Daddy, can we walk around and see the lights up close?"

"I think that's a good idea. Don't you, Beth?"

He was asking her to join them. How could she refuse?

"Awesome." Chloe whirled around and started inside, but stopped to plug in the garland they'd placed on the railing earlier. "We forgot to turn it on. Now it's perfect. Did the lights in the office windows downstairs come on?"

"They should have, provided the timer worked correctly."

Beth slid the throw from her shoulders, only to find Noah there to take it from her. His fingers grazed hers. And she looked into his eyes.

"She's right. This was a perfect evening. The food, the lights, the hostess." He reached out and gently skimmed her cheek with the back of his fingers. "Christmas lights become you."

She held her breath, anticipating his next move. Was he going to kiss her? She hoped so. She couldn't deny her feelings much longer. She'd had feelings for Noah since she'd met him, but what she'd felt back then was a crush. What she was feeling now was grown-up attraction, and she wasn't sure what to do with it.

"Come on, Dad, let's go."

The moment shattered. She set aside her concerns and decided to go with the flow. All she wanted was to walk amid the millions of lights with Noah and Chloe and enjoy the moment. She'd deal with reality tomorrow.

Noah let the noise of the drill drown out his conflicted thoughts as he attached the locking casters to the bottom of the platform he'd built for the large Christmas tree in the show.

He'd retreated here to the workshop right after breakfast, hoping the project would stop the persistent loop of memories that played in his mind. He'd almost kissed her. Twice. His emotions were still firing on all cylinders from his time with Beth last night. His pulse still beat erratically whenever he thought of how close he'd come to kissing her on the balcony.

He'd gotten caught up in the girls' anticipation for the big display of lights, and they hadn't been disappointed. Chloe had been thrilled. Beth had been awestruck, and the glow of the lights along the front of her building had bathed her in a soft light that sent a quiver of attraction along his nerve endings. She was beautiful. Not in a stop-traffic way, but she possessed a sweet and pure loveliness that lingered in your mind forever. Her big hazel eyes drew a man in. Her thick brown hair fell in soft curves to her shoulders, drawing attention to her rosy cheeks and pretty mouth.

He'd wanted nothing more than to take her in his arms and taste her lips. In all the time they'd known each other, he'd never kissed her. Not even a peck on the cheek. If it hadn't been for Chloe's interruption he would have, and if the look in her eyes was any indication, she wouldn't have minded.

It was a good thing he hadn't acted on his impulse. Who knew what kind of Pandora's box of complications that would have unleashed? The evening had chipped away areas of his heart that he'd plastered over long ago, allowing that old dream to break free. Sharing a home-cooked meal in the cozy apartment, laughing with Chloe and watching Beth's delight in everything his daughter said, had filled him with sweet contentment.

Yet instead of following his common sense and going home, he'd agreed to walk around the square. They'd wandered beneath the canopy of lights, marveled at the twinkling storefronts and sipped hot chocolate in the gazebo as they watched the people milling around.

The wind had picked up, putting a bite in the air. He'd taken Beth's hand to keep her warm. He'd wanted the connection. He'd known it was risky but he'd done it anyway, like touching an electrical wire, knowing you'd be injured, but unable to stop yourself. When had he become a masochist?

Pulling off his safety glasses, he pinched the bridge of his nose. Why was it so hard for him to acknowledge the truth? Being with Beth, holding her hand and sharing the brilliant scene with her, had made him feel whole and complete. The only thing that had ever come close to matching that was when he'd held Chloe in his arms for the first time.

"Noah, dear. How's it coming?"

He jerked his thoughts together as his grandmother entered the shop. "Good—the dolly for the tree is done. I just need to paint it, then I can haul it over to the theater."

"I can't thank you enough for lending your skills to my little project."

Noah had to smile. There was nothing little about Gram's projects. Ever. "My pleasure."

"Will you come with me to the storage shed? I have something for you."

Noah followed Gram out back to the old wooden building, waiting while she unlocked the weathered door. Musty air whooshed out of the darkness. The room probably hadn't been opened since Gramps died. He pulled the dangling string to turn on the light, scanning the cluttered interior. "What are we looking for?"

Gram glanced around a moment, then pointed to the section on the right. "There it is." She picked her way toward the dust-covered shapes.

When she pulled the cloth away, he smiled at what was underneath: the scaled-down village pieces his gramps had made for the front lawn decades ago. "What made you think of this? I didn't know these little buildings were still here." His granddad had constructed nearly a dozen miniature Dover buildings and placed them in the front yard. Each building stood between two and three feet high, with the church being the centerpiece. Lit from within, the display had been a charming depiction of a Victorian Dover Christmas.

"I've thought about putting them out again, but it's too much trouble for me." She sidestepped to the piece that was taller than the rest. "I thought with a little freshening up, this might look really nice in your office window."

"The church." Noah lifted the church from amid the other buildings and set it near the door so he could get a better look. Other than a few loose trim pieces and several missing shingles, it was in good shape. "Needs a little attention and a paint job."

Gram touched the steeple. "Sort of like each of us. We need to examine our faith life and make any repairs we've been neglecting." She looked at him.

Was she trying to tell him something?

"Do you think Beth would like it? She has the tree in her window, and you could have the church as your centerpiece. I'm hoping the lights inside still work."

Beth would like it. He had no doubts. "Thanks, Gram. I'll get it in shape this afternoon and take it in tomorrow."

"How's the new client working out? You haven't mentioned him in a few days."

Noah scratched the back of his neck. "He's proving to be a challenge. He likes shortcuts and quick fixes. He's not a fan of adhering to building codes."

"Don't you let him get away with anything."

"I don't intend to. My first priority is to keep people safe. Even if they don't realize they need safety."

He carried the church back into the workshop and set it on the bench, his gaze drifting to the tree stand. His workshop was being taken over by projects for Beth. His gram may be the source of the work, but the one who had to be pleased was Beth. And he wanted to please her.

He was doomed. That cement he'd stepped in had hardened, and he'd need a jackhammer and a lot of determination to chip his way free.

Beth stepped inside the senior center on Church Street and took a deep, fortifying breath. Today was her first dance class, and her stomach was fluttering as if a swarm of butterflies were inside. She'd checked with Pete and gone over her routine. He'd approved it, but he'd advised her to go slowly and keep in mind the limitations of her older students.

Her gaze scanned the room for Evelyn, but it was the familiar face of Millie Tedrow she saw first. The former librarian had introduced her to many wonderful books. When Beth hadn't been dancing, she'd been reading.

"Bethany my dear, you look wonderful." She came toward her, arms outstretched. "We are so excited about your class. Evelyn is already upstairs." She led the way through a space filled with comfy couches, recliners, game tables and a big-screen television. To the rear was a large gleaming kitchen and eating area.

"This place is amazing."

Millie stopped in the back beside a staircase and a small elevator. "It is. Lots to do. The lower level is an activities room, and upstairs is the craft and exercise space. There's an apartment on the third floor that the director, Greta Rogers, lives in. We're not open round-the-clock, but it's good to have someone on the premises at all times."

"Greta was very helpful in organizing this dance class." Beth followed the woman up the stairs, pleased to see she hadn't taken the elevator.

"She was sorry she couldn't be here today. She wanted to meet you in person."

On the second floor Millie walked through a narrow hallway past bathrooms, then into a large open space with wood floors and large windows looking out onto the square. Nearly a dozen women smiled and waved as she entered. Evelyn hurried forward.

"We can't wait to get started."

The next forty-five minutes flew by. Evelyn introduced her to everyone, and Beth took a few minutes to learn about their dance backgrounds and what they hoped to accomplish by learning to dance. She took her time demonstrating simple basic steps of tap and ballet, keeping a close eye on the exercise. Today's class had been designed for ambulatory seniors. If there was enough interest, she'd look into starting a chair class for those who weren't able to stand for long periods of time and those in wheelchairs.

Everyone was eager and willing to try each move.

A couple of ladies teased her about the tights and leotard she'd worn today. She explained that the outfit made it easier to see how they were supposed to stand and move.

"I hope we don't have to get some of those things to wear," one woman joked.

A heavyset lady chimed in. "I don't mind getting them, but I could never get 'em up."

Beth joined in the laughter. It didn't take long to see the potential for smaller, more diverse classes. The varying levels of ability and interest would be challenging, and the thought fueled her energy. If this dance class took off, she could see bringing in another instructor to help. It was an idea she'd like to present to the center's director.

"Great workout. We'll slowly build up to doing more as we go."

Echoes of conversation bounced around the high ceilings as the seniors drifted out of the room. Some grumbled, some claimed they felt better already and a few decided they didn't like to dance at all. None of that discouraged her. She knew if they'd really enjoyed it, they would return. The most amazing part of the afternoon was how much *she* had enjoyed the class. She couldn't wait to tell Evelyn and thank her for the suggestion.

But when she glanced around the room, her gaze landed on Evelyn's grandson instead. Noah stood at the edge of the room, one shoulder resting against the doorjamb, arms crossed over his chest and one hip cocked in a purely masculine pose. Her mouth went dry. Sometimes she wished he'd stayed skinny. This attractive, mature version had way too much heart appeal.

"You looked like you were having fun."

He came toward her, a small smile lighting his blue eyes. A soft sigh escaped her throat. He'd always had the most knee-weakening smile. Whenever he'd flash that row of white teeth, it would bring out a deep crease on one side of his mouth. She'd always thought he looked very roguish. Like a tall, dark pirate, or a dangerous sea captain. But she'd been reading a lot of historical romance novels back then.

She cleared her throat. "I was. Are you here to learn to dance?"

He shrugged, the twinkle in his eyes flashing. "That's an intriguing idea."

Their eyes locked, trapping the breath in her throat. Was he imagining the same thing she was? The two of them in each other's arms, waltzing in the starlight?

"Oh, my." Evelyn dabbed at her neck with a towel as she walked over to them. "I'd forgotten how strenuous dancing could be. Just those few steps had me huffing." She patted her grandson's arm. "But all this exertion is more fun when you do it with friends. Speaking of fun, we're going to decorate the center's Christmas tree tomorrow, and we could use some assistance. Even putting ornaments on trees isn't as easy as it used to be. You two would be a big help."

Beth suspected some matchmaking tactics at work here. Noah would never refuse his grandmother, and she couldn't turn down a plea to help these sweet people. "I'd love to." She looked at Noah and raised her chin, daring him to refuse. She allowed a small smirk to lift her mouth, and she stifled a giggle at the resigned look in his eyes. He was aware of the maneuvering taking place.

"Sure. What time?"

"Afternoon, then Chloe can help, too."

Beth's affection for Evelyn tripled in that moment. She was doing what Beth couldn't—finding more ways for her to be with Noah and Chloe.

Noah glanced over at his grandmother as he drove her home after exercise class. The small, self-satisfied smile told him all he needed to know. "What are you up to?"

She faced him, her expression one of pure innocence. "Excuse me?"

"Don't try your mind tricks on me. You keep finding ways to put me and Beth together. You need to stop. There is nothing between us, and there never will be."

"Oh, I'm sure of that."

"What does that mean?"

"Well, you are a down-to-earth, no-nonsense kind of guy, like your father, and Beth is a sprig of spring flowers, a dandelion puff on a warm breeze, a sparkle of sunlight on the water."

Noah shook his head. "And she disappears when the dancing muse summons her."

His gram waved off his words. "Noah, you are assuming way too much. Have you talked to her about that time?"

"Actually, we have. The bottom line is her career was more important than our friendship." *And she didn't love me.*

"That sounds more like Yvonne than Beth. Did you ever tell her how you felt?"

"No. There was no point."

"If you never told her, then how can you hold her responsible for something she didn't even know about?"

"We were talking about your clumsy attempts at matchmaking."

"Were we? When? Oh, look. We're home. Thank you for picking me up, dear. I'm going to get supper started."

Before he could respond, Gram was out of the car and hurrying to the porch. For an old lady with arthritis, she moved fast. He sat in the car a moment. Gram was right about one thing. Beth was all the things she'd mentioned. He was acutely aware of it whenever she was near. Watching her work with the seniors had lifted another layer away from his emotional barrier. She'd been gentle and considerate as she helped them with their movements, completely shattering the image of the indifferent woman he wanted her to be. If she was cold and callous he could dismiss her easily, keep his wall of doubt intact. But if she was the warm and caring woman he remembered, then he was in danger of falling in love with her again.

Gram was right. How could he hold her responsible for his feelings? Yes, she'd broken his heart, but he wasn't the first guy to be rejected. Yes, she'd ignored friends and family after she left home, but he was guilty of the same neglect. When he'd moved to California, his grandparents had frequently complained that he rarely called or came home to see them. He'd been busy, starting his career and his life. Could he blame Beth for doing the same thing?

But what about when she left? And what about Chloe? After Thanksgiving with the Montgomerys decorating the windows and the lighting event, she was in love with Beth. She'd even ordered a poster of Beth to put on her bedroom wall.

He had to remember it was his job as her father to protect her from getting hurt. She was getting too enamored of Beth. It was time to pull back and put some distance between them. Once the show was over, he'd put an end to the dance lessons and sign her up for more soccer. She should be ready to play indoor soccer for the winter. That should give her plenty to focus on.

Yet deep down, he knew it wasn't that simple. Chloe gave all of her little heart to those she loved, and her trust, as well. He used to be that way. A couple of classes at the school of hard knocks had cured him. Now he realized he wanted to love and trust again.

Except the risk was too high. He couldn't face another rejection.

The afternoon light was already fading, casting downtown Dover into dull shadows. Usually the early darkness of winter dragged Beth down, but nothing could diminish her excitement today. She'd started decorating her apartment last night, placing many of her sister's lovely items around on shelves and end tables. She'd even added a few of her own touches with candles she'd picked up the other day. For the first time in years, she was embracing the holiday and looking forward to helping the people at the senior center decorate their tree.

Strange how she'd been surrounded by the extravagant holiday displays and events in New York City for years, but she'd hadn't experienced this kind of childlike excitement since she was little. Or the growing sense of satisfaction. Since her first class with the seniors, she'd received a dozen calls telling her how much fun they'd had and how they couldn't wait for the next class. They were all looking forward to the tree-decorating party today and never failed to remind her to bring Noah along.

Picking up her purse, she locked up and went next door. She noticed the addition to the window immediately as she entered Noah's front office. He was seated at the desk, but she strode past him to the display window.

"Where did you find this precious church?" She stroked the roofline, then bent down to peek in the small windows that had been painted to look like stained glass.

"Gramps made it. He had a whole village of houses and buildings he'd put on the front lawn for Christmas. Gram thought it would look good in the window."

"I remember that little town. I used to wish I could shrink down like Alice in Wonderland so I could go inside each building. This is the perfect touch for our windows. Does it light up?" She spun and smiled at him, only to receive a deep frown in response.

"It will. I have to pick up a bulb."

He lowered his gaze as if not wanting to look at her. She tried to ignore the sharp twinge in her throat. "Perfect. We might just have a chance at winning a prize in the window-decorating contest this weekend."

Noah shifted in his chair. Something had made him very uncomfortable. Her? She didn't understand him at all. The mixed signals were driving her crazy.

"Are you ready to help decorate the tree?"

"Sorry, but I have to work. I have a stack of inspection reports to finalize."

She moved toward him, only to see him brace. What had she done now? "Noah, your gram and the seniors are counting on you to help."

He avoided looking at her and shuffled the papers on his desk. "There should be plenty of people there."

Beth stepped to the edge of the desk, her fingers resting on the top instead of around his neck, despite her temptation to put them there. "What about Chloe?"

"Gram picked her up from school. They should already be at the center. You'd better go on."

"Noah, what's bothering you? Have I said something or done something to upset you? If so, I'm sorry. I can't fix it if you don't tell me what's wrong."

He looked at her with eyes filled with a strange mixture of sadness and confusion. "It's not you, it's—" He paused for a second, then inhaled a deep breath and squared his shoulders. "Like I said. I've got work to do."

His tone said the subject was closed. "Fine." She strode to the door, then spun around. "You know you're letting Chloe down the same way her mother does. You told her you'd help decorate, but at the last minute, you're backing out. For *work*. How can you justify disappointing her this way?"

Noah didn't meet her gaze. He stared resolutely at the papers on his desk. With a loud huff, she pulled open the door and left.

Men. They said one thing but did another. When would she learn that lesson?

Chapter Eight

Noah's office door closed with a sharp click, leaving him in silence to confront things he'd rather avoid. Like the way his emotions were constantly swinging between his need to protect his daughter and his growing feelings for Beth. He should have anticipated Beth stopping by. He should have known she'd want to go together.

He gazed at the wooden church in the display window. He'd been ridiculously pleased that she liked it. And pleasing her had become one of his goals. But alongside that emotion flashed a warning sign, reminding him to maintain a clear distance and protect his heart.

Since she'd come home to Dover, he'd been forced to adjust his opinions of Beth and view the past through a more mature lens. Nothing was as cut-and-dried as it appeared. He shouldn't have interpreted her sudden departure as a personal rejection. And he should have tried harder to find out the truth. But his ego had been bruised, and he'd made assumptions. He hated to think he'd been that shallow and selfish, but at eighteen he'd thought he understood the world. Now, at thirty-one, he knew better. Though he still wasn't clear how his confusion over her gift had given her the impression he didn't care about her.

His cell buzzed, and Chloe's picture appeared on the screen. "Hey, princess. Everything all right?"

"Daddy, where are you? Gram and I are here, and so is Miss Beth. It's time to decorate the tree. Hurry up or you'll miss it."

Noah rubbed his forehead. How could he spend time with Beth, knowing the constant exposure would only peel away another layer of his heart? Their truce should have made being with her easier. Instead it had only increased his longing to reestablish the friendship they'd once had.

No. He needed to stick to his plan. Steer clear and keep his distance.

"Sorry, but I have to work today. You and Gram have fun, and tell me all about it over supper tonight."

The disappointment in his daughter's voice as she said goodbye spilled like hot lead along each of his nerve endings.

After hanging up, he rested his elbows on the desk, hands fisted against his mouth as waves of guilt crashed against his mind. Beth was right. He was doing what Yvonne always did. Putting a job before family. Something he swore he'd never do. And not because he loved work, but because he was afraid.

Shoving away from his desk, he snatched his jacket from the back of his chair, locked up and headed across the courthouse park to the senior center. Warmth and the mouthwatering aroma of fresh popcorn greeted him as he stepped inside. The large tree in front of the window was surrounded by people when he arrived. It looked like his skills wouldn't be needed after all. Chloe spotted him and dashed across the room full tilt, throwing herself into his arms and knocking him backward. He scooped her up and held her close. At nine she was too big to hold, but he relished the feel of her in his arms, hugging his neck.

"Daddy, I'm so glad you came."

"Me, too, princess."

"Come on, we need your help with the extra lights."

Beth turned as he approached the tree, and the smile on her lovely face wiped all doubts from his mind. This is where he wanted to be. Working beside her and his daughter.

The sweet melody of "I'll Be Home for Christmas" that had been playing when he came in gave way to "Little Saint Nick." He chuckled as some of the seniors started to move to the upbeat tune and sing along.

"Chester Floyd, get your hands out of the popcorn." Gram wagged a finger at the stocky gentleman. "That's for stringing on the tree."

Beth's soft laughter drew his gaze to her. Her smile was bright and mischievous. "Let that be a lesson to you. No munching the decorations."

"I'm glad I'm not Chester."

"Daddy, you need to hang this up 'cause you're tall." Chloe hurried toward him, her hands overflowing with a pile of popcorn garland. It took him a moment to locate the end, then he tucked it in the back of the tree near the top and slowly draped it across the branches.

"It's so pretty, Daddy. Isn't this fun?"

He looked down at his child. The dreamy glow in her blue eyes was the most beautiful thing he'd ever seen. Beth stepped to Chloe's side and slipped her arm across her shoulders, a happy smile bringing a pink flush to her cheeks. He was glad he'd changed his mind and come. Sharing Chloe's and Beth's delight was too precious a moment to miss for work.

While the next strand of popcorn was being assembled, he and Beth began removing the lids from the boxes of ornaments stacked on a table. He watched her face fill with delight as she opened each box. She looked happy and content. But for how long? She caught him staring and held his gaze, smiling deep into his eyes.

"I'm glad you changed your mind about coming."

"You were right. I was behaving exactly like Yvonne. I swore I'd never let her down."

"You know that's an impossible goal."

"Yeah. But a father can dream."

She faced him, raising her eyebrows. "Oh. So you *do* have dreams. I knew it."

He smiled, taking the bulb from her hand and letting his fingers brush against hers. What would she say if he told her he was living a dream right now? Being with her and Chloe, performing a holiday ritual like a normal family, was a dream he'd held since his parents died. But she knew that already. He'd told her long ago. Did she remember?

Beth lifted a glass ballerina ornament from the box. "Oh, how sweet. Chloe, look what I found." She hurried over to the tree, and he watched the two of them search out the perfect spot to hang the ornament, leaving him to second-guess his decision. Had he just made another big mistake by coming to help? In making Chloe happy in the short term, and sharing more time with Beth, he may have set them both up for a bigger disappointment down the road when she left.

How was a father supposed to know what was right?

Beth watched the dancers as they went through their steps for the scene from *The Nutcracker*. Allison had chosen the scene when Clara receives her gift and combined it with a few more iconic Victorian holiday scenes.

When the music ended, Beth moved up onstage. "Great job, everyone. Now remember, we'll be practicing every night between now and the performance. I know that's a lot to ask, but we all want this show to be the very best. It'll all be worth it when you hear that applause. And speaking of that, while this is a performance, remember that we are also trying to show not only the earthly joy of Christmas, but also the joyous miracle of Emmanuel. God with us. Here as a human baby. So when the applause starts, remember it's not only for you, but for Him, as well. Take a break, and we'll run through the final number one more time."

Beth looked over her notes, jotting down a few thoughts on how to improve the number. A swell of happy satisfaction rose up through her body, bringing a smile she didn't try to hide. She was beginning to think Miss Evelyn was right about God having more than one blessing in store for each of His children. Taking this job had already blessed her in ways she never could have imagined.

"I'd like to speak with you, Miss Montgomery."

She looked up as Beulah Jenson approached, with a tearful girl in tow. Her daughter, Mindy, was dancing the role of Clara in the *Nutcracker* segment. If there was one sour note in the show, it was Mrs. Jenson. The woman found fault with every direction Beth or Jen gave, and tested her self-control to the limit.

"I'm afraid your practice schedule is too strenuous for Mindy. From here on I'll only bring her to the important rehearsals."

Beth struggled to keep the irritation from her tone as she spoke. "Mrs. Jenson, Mindy has a key role in this production. She needs to be here for each rehearsal in case we have to make any changes."

"If you ask me, there are far too many changes. You may be a professional, but Mindy isn't, and I don't appreciate the way you work her beyond her capabilities. The routines were perfectly fine until you showed up and complicated everything. I think it's best we let her part be taken over by her understudy."

Beth blinked. Was she serious? "She doesn't have an understudy. This is a little theater production, and the performers are here because they want to be."

"Well, we no longer want to *be*." She whirled, grabbed her sobbing daughter's hand and marched out.

Beth clutched her notes to her chest. Great. One of the main performers had quit. Mindy was hardly the best dancer, but she knew her part. Beth's confidence sagged. She thought she'd been doing a good job. Everyone was tired, but no one had balked at the extra practices. "What am I going to do now?"

"Don't worry about it." Jen came and stood at her side. "I've been expecting this from the beginning. Stage mother."

"I'm sorry. I guess I'm better at performing than directing and choreographing."

"You're great at both. Don't let her get you down. Beulah has a reputation for being difficult."

"That doesn't solve the problem of losing our Clara."

"No, but we'll think of something. Maybe one of the older girls could take the part?"

Beth stared at the stage, mentally running through the routine and reimagining the sequence. Excitement sent her pulse racing as an idea began to form. "What about three Clara's?"

"What?"

"I've been teaching Chloe and my niece and her friend basic ballet. What if we had the three girls dance the part together? They already know some easy steps. We could dress them alike, pick up two more small nutcrackers and present them as triplets."

Jen nodded. "It might be cute. See if you can set it up."

A squiggle of excitement zinged along her nerves. She was certain Abby and Hannah would love the idea. Chloe, too, but she wasn't sure how Noah would react. Giving Chloe dance lessons as incentive to do her PT exercises was a far cry from actually performing on-stage. "I don't know if Noah will like the idea. He may not want Chloe in the show."

"Why not? His gram is putting it on."

Beth frowned. "It's complicated. But maybe I can get his gram on our side. And make sure he knows we're in a difficult position with the show only a week away."

Jen squeezed her hand. "If I remember correctly, you can be very persuasive when you set your mind to something. We make a good team. I look forward to the next production."

Beth looked at the warm smile on Jen's face, her memory flashing back to when they'd shared so many happy times. "I must confess I'm enjoying this more than I thought I would. My life has been so set in one direction that I'd forgotten how much fun other things can be, and how important old friendships are. I'm sorry I failed to keep in touch over the years."

"Don't be silly. It's what happens after school. We all go on with our lives. I thought about you often, and I'm so proud of what you accomplished. The friendship never went away, Beth. It was held in a special place in my heart, waiting to be dusted off and polished up again."

Beth gathered up her belongings, wondering if her friendship with Noah could be polished up, or if it was simply too late. The truce had eased the tension between them, making it easier to be together. But Noah still carried his shield at his side, ready to raise it without warning.

She knew he was trying to protect himself from being hurt again, but how could they ever move forward if he didn't drop his guard? Maybe he didn't want to. Maybe she was indulging in wishful thinking again. Wanting him to care because she did.

She knew he was attracted to her. The sparks between them were too strong to ignore. But was that mere chemistry, old emotions stirred to life again? Or was it something more? Something that could become real?

She grabbed her tablet and made a few notes about the changes she had to make. She had no time to worry about what Noah did or did not feel.

* * *

Noah set the screw in place, pressed the trigger on the drill and drove it into the wood. A second screw secured the table leg in place. He tightened the other screws before setting the small table upright, confident it wouldn't wobble during the *Night Before Christmas* act.

He straightened and removed the drill bit. Despite telling himself not to, his gaze sought out Beth, who was standing in the aisle talking with the mother of one of the children. He forced himself to look away and gather up his tools. His feelings for Beth were growing each day. He still couldn't bring himself to believe that Beth would stay in Dover. Given the chance, she'd dance her way out of his life at the first opportunity.

Yet he knew she was enjoying teaching the girls and working with the seniors at the center. He'd seen her gentleness toward his gram and the others in her class. Here at the rehearsals, she glowed with energy and enthusiasm, and he was confronted hourly with his daughter's adoration for Beth.

She had a lot to offer their small hometown. Her heart for others was evident in everything she did. That was the Beth he remembered. The one that still called to him from the far recesses of his mind. But was it enough? Could teaching others to dance take the place of doing it herself? Could she ever completely let go of her lifelong dream?

"Noah, do you have a moment?"

He spun, nearly bumping into the object of his thoughts. "Sure." She was holding her tablet. He frowned. What did she want constructed now?

"I need one more rather large prop, and I was hoping you could throw it together."

Why did everyone think that building things was just a matter of throwing some lumber together? "You do realize that the show is next week."

"I know, but we've had a change in one of the numbers. Mindy Jenson pulled out—or rather, her mother pulled her out. Which means I have to restage the number, and I had an idea."

He didn't even try to hide the groan, but he tempered it with a wary smile. "What is it?"

"I need a giant nutcracker."

"What?"

She hastened to explain. "It doesn't have to be elaborate or anything, but it needs to be about eight feet tall and about three to four feet wide." She rotated the tablet so he could see her sketch.

The design looked like an actual nutcracker with tubular arms, a tall hat, full body and long legs ending in boots on a platform. "Beth, that would take weeks to construct, not to mention the time to figure the angles, the amount of wood and other materials."

"I thought you were a structural engineer?"

"I am."

"So make a structure."

Her eyes twinkled, and he realized she was teasing him. "Very funny. Now what do you really want?"

"A big nutcracker, but it can be a one-dimensional flat one. Eric will paint in all the details, but it's an important prop because it'll be the one your daughter will be dancing around."

"What are you talking about?"

Beth clutched her tablet to her chest like a protective

shield. "Since we've lost our Clara, I'm going to replace her with three Clara's. Abby, Hannah and Chloe."

Not what he'd expected. He shook his head. "I don't know about that."

"As you pointed out, we only have one week until opening night. I'm improvising. Besides, I know the girls will love the idea. Please consider letting Chloe be in the number. It's only one performance, not a life-long contract."

She had a point, but what if she got a taste of performing and liked it? He met her gaze, trying to ignore the hopeful glint in her pretty eyes. He knew once his daughter heard the idea, there'd be no way he could tell her no. "All right." He pointed to the tablet. "How soon do you need it?"

"The sooner the better. Thank you, Noah. For letting Chloe dance and for the prop. Is it all right if I call her now?"

"Sure." He nodded, then watched her hurry off. He needed to figure out when he'd lost control of his life.

Chapter Nine

Noah stared at the sketches Beth had emailed him of her nutcracker idea. One, a complicated three-dimensional one. The other, a simple flat one in the shape of a nutcracker. With so little time left until opening night, he really didn't have time to do more than cut out the shape and get it back to the theater so Eric could paint it.

However, what he wanted to do was surprise Beth with the giant nutcracker she'd teased him with. He could imagine her shock and delight when he brought it into the theater. Ideas on how to create it had started forming in his mind from the moment she'd suggested it. He'd worked out a simple design, but he'd have to rely on Eric to make it look realistic.

He had plenty of lumber, and the rest he was hoping to find in the storage shed. When it came to building materials and supplies, Gramps had been a pack rat. He believed sooner or later he'd find a use for all the things he'd saved.

Pulling the shed key from the hook beside the door, he let himself in, heading toward the large assortment

of poles, pipes and other odd-shaped pieces. After se-
lecting a small plastic box, several lengths of PVC
pipe and a bucket, he set them beside the door. As
he reached for the string to turn off the light, a small
wooden object caught his attention. His treasure box.

It was the size of a shoe box. His gramps had built
it for him as a Christmas gift when he was ten. He and
his parents had been living in Florida at the time, and
he'd been fascinated with pirates and wanted a place
to keep his valuables. Over time the box had held a
variety of important items. His throat thickened as he
thought about the last items of value he'd placed in the
box. Slowly he raised the lid, his gaze zeroing in on
the small white box in the middle. Beth's graduation
gift to him. His hand shook as he reached for it. What
had she written on the back? She claimed it was nothing but a friendly sentiment.

The oddly shaped emblem on the key ring glinted
in the light when he removed the lid. Nestled upon the
white batting inside was what he could clearly see now
was a heart, shaped as if it had been gently tugged to
one side, distorting its shape. He swallowed against the
dryness in his throat, then flipped over the charm, his
breath catching as he read the words engraved there.

Noah, every time you touch this you'll be touching my heart. Love, Beth

Love? He read the words again, trying to understand. The sentiment was from someone who cared—
deeply. Not a casual friend. Had she cared? Had she
loved him?

His gaze landed on the other small box in the chest.

The gift he'd selected for her. Beneath the blue box was a faded paper. His speech. The one he'd never gotten to deliver.

Noah gripped the key ring in his palm, wrapping his fingers around it and feeling the sharp edges dig into his skin. What did he do now? Did he tell Beth and ask her what she meant? Did he dare hope that she'd been confessing her love for him that day? Or was he reading too much into a few simple words?

Even if she'd meant the words, even if she'd given him the gift and revealed her feelings, when the call from Forsythe had come she would have gone anyway. Dancing had been her whole life then. Still was.

He didn't have the energy to try to figure it out now. Shoving the key ring into his pants pocket, he gathered up the materials and headed back to the shop. Working with his hands was a good way to sort out his thoughts and come to a decision.

Or even better, avoid one.

The sun was barely up the next morning when Beth switched on the lights in her small studio. Sleep had been impossible. Dark and disturbing dreams had awakened her several times during the night, leaving her shaken and filled with a chilling sense of abandonment. Her body ached, and the thought of doing her exercises and ballet warm-up dragged her down. She didn't have the energy for either. But she would do them just the same.

She pulled off her jacket and changed into comfy pants and a tank top before starting her physical therapy exercises. She ran through them with ease, then moved to the mirrored wall, intending to begin her ballet warm-up. She stopped, a hard knot lodging in her throat as she stared at her reflection. Why bother? Her life as a professional ballerina with the Forsythe Company had ended with a swipe of a pen.

She'd met with Blake Prescott yesterday, the family attorney, and gone over her contract, ultimately deciding to terminate her association with the ballet. She had nothing to gain by holding out the last two months. It was a scary prospect, and she suspected her decision was the cause of her nightmares. She had no idea what she would do going forward.

But for now, she would go through her ballet warm-up. It's what she did when she hurt or was lonely or confused. She danced. Some people sought solace in a bar. She found it at a different barre.

Pushing the play button, she started her favorite CD of praise music. The familiar songs gave her a measure of comfort, and allowed her to reconnect with the artist she'd once been. The opening strains washed over her as she grasped the barre and prepared, acutely aware of the alignment of her hips, legs and turnout. Slow *tendu*. First position. *Demi plié* and stretch. Four-count *relevé*…

The warm-up was so engrained into her muscle memory that it had become a struggle to hold back from throwing herself into it fully. Her knee wasn't ready for a *grande plié*, but she was close.

At thirty years old, she was well aware she was entering the last phase of her career. She was also aware of the younger dancers waiting in the wings, eager to jump into her place. She refocused on her warm-up. *Plié, eleve*, point toes, front, back, side, change position. It was as natural as breathing. She raised her arm, letting it float on the air with the music as she stretched. It felt so familiar, so right. She missed it so much.

An hour later, drained yet exhilarated, she downed several gulps of water and smiled at her reflection. She'd pushed it a little more today. The pain was easing with each workout, and she felt herself growing stronger.

Fueled with confidence, she decided to try a little center work. Stepping to the middle of the room, she balanced, positioned her arms and raised her right leg out to the side, only to wobble and lose her balance. Three more tries only led to frustration. The sense of lightness and control she always experienced was missing, replaced with a feeling of clumsiness. Nothing was the same anymore. Not her body, not her proficiency level, not even herself.

Taking a moment to collect herself, she started toward the small sofa, her gaze landing on the pair of worn pink *pointe* shoes hanging on the wall. Gently she took them in her hands, overcome with poignant memories. They were her last pair before she'd left for New York. The ones she'd worn as she'd practiced for her audition to the Forsythe Company. She'd danced her very best, but it hadn't been good enough. Until another position had opened up, and her prayers had been answered and her dream realized.

Beth sank down onto the small sofa, her fingers stroking the worn satin. She'd left Dover with wings on her feet. She'd worked harder than anyone, rising through the ranks from corps de ballet to demi-soloist and eventually principal dancer, achieving everything she'd set out to.

Noah's question reverberated in her mind. But what had it cost her? A friend who felt rejected. A mother who'd needed to hear from her daughter, a family she'd barely seen since she was eighteen. The memory of Chloe's sorrowful expression when her mother had failed to live up to her promise surfaced. Is that what her mother and father had experienced? Sadness and disappointment?

Leaning back against the cushion, she clutched the shoes to her chest as stark realization forced its way into her mind. This wasn't about dancing, this was about her. The truth about her life was coming to the surface, forcing her to confront her sins and short-comings.

When had she become so indifferent to others' feelings?

She knew the answer. It had been that night she'd left Dover. Realizing Noah didn't love her had shaken her foundation. From then on, becoming a professional dancer had changed from being a dream to a necessity, a way to prove her worth to herself and to him.

Once she left Dover, her life had been all about becoming the best dancer she could be. Living her dream. She had shoved everyone aside in her drive to succeed. There'd been moments when she'd looked up and realized she was alone. No close friends, a family far away, no special someone. But then the dance would call, and she'd plunge into it and forget everything else.

Her dad had always stressed faith first, but she'd never really understood what he'd meant. She was beginning to now. She was coming to see that she'd placed things in her life in the wrong order. A swell of shame and regret formed deep inside. Her life was out of balance.

Her mom was right. She'd been holding on to something that was never going to happen. She had to change. If she didn't, she'd end up chasing everyone in her life away—again. She didn't want to lose Noah or Chloe. They'd become too much a part of her life now.

Did she have the courage? She couldn't do it alone.

She looked at the middle of the room. A few moments ago she'd tried to balance on her good leg without support. It should have been easy. But her body was out of balance, too. She needed the barre to steady her. And she needed something more than her own determination to balance her life. She *had* to reset her priorities. Put God first. His hand should be what she grasped for security, not the wooden beam against the wall.

Lord, forgive me. I don't want to be that person. Help me find a way to reconnect with those I love and balance my life. I want You first in my life.

Her dream was over. She had to face it. God gave her what she dreamed of, but He never said it would last forever.

Clutching the shoes to her chest, she grieved the passing of a dream.

Beth stood onstage the next night, staring in disbelief at the giant nutcracker Noah had delivered that evening. She'd been expecting a flat in the shape of a nutcracker. Instead he presented her with a three-dimensional eight-foot version, complete with tall hat, round arms and legs, and a square wooden body on a rolling platform. The sections were a mismatch of materials, but Eric could transform it into a spectacular sight. "When did you do this? It's amazing."

He grinned, his eyes bright with pride. "I realized it wouldn't be all that difficult to make a large one if I used PVC pipe for arms and legs and kept the body square. Once I started, it took on a life of its own. Of course, Eric will have to use his skill to make it look like an actual nutcracker."

"You put so much work into this. Thank you. This is going to transform the entire number."

He shrugged, his expression revealing his embarrassment. "Well, it is my daughter's shining moment after all."

Unable to contain her delight, she slipped her arms around his neck and gave him a kiss on the cheek. As she pulled away, her attention landed on his mouth, only inches from hers if she shifted just a bit. Heart pounding, she moved her hand from his shoulder to his jaw. It was warm and strong and slightly scratchy from end-of-day stubble. She dared to look into his eyes and saw her own desire reflected in the blue depths.

It hit her then that they were standing in the open, where anyone and everyone could see them. She swallowed, tucked her hair behind her ears and stepped back. "Thank you, Noah. It's amazing."

"I'm glad you like it." He held her gaze a moment, searching her face. "You've changed."

She frowned, glancing down at her outfit. What was he talking about?

"You look different. Your eyes aren't shadowed anymore. Your smile isn't restrained. What happened?"

Was her transformation so apparent? But then, Noah would notice things like that. Perhaps this was the opening she'd been waiting for. The time to have a talk about what really had been going on in her heart back then. "You're right. Something has changed. Maybe we can talk about it after rehearsal?"

"I'd like that. I have something to tell you, too. And I have some questions."

Questions? That dimmed her mood a bit. But once they sat down and talked it out, she knew things would be better, and hopefully they could admit the attraction between them and move forward. After all her soul-searching the other night, there'd been one more truth she'd had to face and accept. She loved Noah. Always had. Always would.

A knot formed in her abdomen. What about now? Was she just seeing what she wanted? Was this attraction only on her part?

Beth carried the warmth of Noah's touch with her the rest of the rehearsal. Their relationship had changed over the last weeks. Working together on the show and the props had eased them back into their comfortable friendship. More importantly—and disturbingly—the attraction between them had heated up. Her heart was already in danger, but now the sparks between them were zinging whenever they were close.

Noah stopped at her side, his smile warm and affectionate, his blue eyes filled with tenderness. "May I walk you home?"

"I'd like that."

Outside, Beth pulled her coat a little closer. The weather was unusually cold for southern Mississippi. Thankfully the forecast called for a warm-up tomorrow. She didn't mind the chill, especially when Noah took her hand in his.

"Thank you again for the wonderful nutcracker. It's amazing."

"This is an important holiday event. A guy shouldn't skimp when his three favorite women are involved."

"Three?"

"Gram, Chloe and—" He squeezed her hand. "You."

She couldn't misunderstand the tone of affection in his voice or the look in his eyes. Now would be a good time to tell him about the inscription. But where did she start? "I'm glad you let Chloe do the number. She's very excited, and she's working very hard to learn the routine."

"She practices at home all the time. Every time I turn around, I'm running into her."

"You're a great dad, Noah." Inhaling a fortifying breath, she plunged ahead. "Have you ever thought about getting married again?" She sensed his surprise.

"No. I don't think I'm very good at the marriage thing."

"I don't believe that. Any woman would be blessed to have you for a husband. You're a good man."

"Charlie Brown."

She chuckled and moved closer to his side. "Well, you are."

"What about you? Why haven't you taken the plunge? I'm sure you had plenty of chances. You must have had guys falling at your feet wanting to date the beautiful ballerina."

A shadow settled over her happy mood. This wasn't the topic she wanted to discuss, but maybe it was time to share that heartache with him. "There was a man. His name was Ivan and he was a guest dancer from Russia, very charming and sophisticated. We started dating. I was head over heels in love with him, and I got carried away with my emotions. Everything was fine until I told him I was pregnant. Then he moved on to the next girl and the next city and left me to deal with a miscarriage all by myself. I never saw him again."

Noah stopped and faced her, pulling her into his embrace. "Oh, my Beth. I'm sorry you had to go through that alone."

Beth allowed the warmth and protection of his arms to soothe her, wishing she could turn to him with her worries every day. His Beth. That's all she'd ever wanted to be.

"What about your family?"

"I couldn't tell them. I was too ashamed. I was still trying to figure out what to do when I lost the baby."

Noah gently set her away, looking deep into her eyes. "Is that why you left the table so suddenly on Thanksgiving Day after Abby announced the new baby?"

She nodded. "I'm happy for them, but it only reminded me of the big hole in my own life. Sorry to dump this on you."

They'd stopped at the apartment door. Noah tilted her chin upward as he looked deep into her eyes. "Don't be. I'm glad you told me. You used to tell me all your deepest secrets."

She touched his lips with her fingertips. "That's because you always understood. I wish we'd been friends then. I was so scared and alone."

"You deserve so much better."

"I'm not so sure." She touched her leg. "My injury wasn't entirely an accident. I'd been pushing myself beyond my limits since I lost the baby. I didn't know what else to do. I didn't want to tell my parents. Then Dad died suddenly, and I couldn't tell Mom, so I buried myself in my career. It's all I had. Sometimes I think that's all I am. A dancer."

"You're wrong. You're more than a dancer. Yes, you devoted yourself to your art, but when you came out of that studio you were always doing things for others. Remember we served meals at the community Christmas dinner? You helped with a habitat house and collected toys for the kids at Christmas. And now you're teaching the people at the senior center, working with the theater and teaching Chloe and her friends. You have more to offer than a brief time in the spotlight."

His support touched her deeply, and gave her hope for their relationship. "Do you think so? Because you were right. Something has changed, and I want to tell you about it. Can you stay for a while? I'll fix coffee."

"Make a big pot. We have a lot of things to discuss."

Up in her apartment, Beth poured a cup of coffee, mentally rehearsing what she would say to Noah. As she set his mug before him, the doorbell chimed. *Who could possibly be stopping by at this hour?*

"Are you expecting someone?"

"No. It's too late for Mom to come by, and the boys never come here unless invited." Moving to the security screen that allowed a view of the door below, she frowned when she saw a man standing there. He turned his head. She inhaled a quick breath. What was he doing here?

She glanced at Noah. "It's a friend from New York." She buzzed the man in and waited at the top of the stairs as he walked up, conscious of Noah standing protectively at her side.

"Who is this guy?"

The man obviously overheard because he reached the top of the steps, pulled Beth into a bear hug and announced, "This guy is the man who's going to change her life."

Beth saw the muscles in Noah's jaw flex rapidly and his lips press into a hard line. She shoved her guest away, putting distance between them. "Kurt, what are you doing here?"

"I was passing through and wanted to say hello." He stepped close again and draped an arm across her shoulders. She moved out of his reach. The man had always been far too touchy-feely for her liking. "No one just passes through Dover. It's not on the way to anywhere."

"You telling me? It's barely on the map. Seriously, I'm on my way to New Orleans and I wanted to see you in person."

"How did you find me?"

"Seems everyone in this town knows who you are."

Beth became aware of Noah standing close, as if to protect her from an unknown threat. "Noah, this is Kurt Townsend from the Forsythe Ballet Company. Kurt, Noah Carlisle. An old friend."

The men nodded. Neither one offered a hand to shake. Beth gritted her teeth. Of all the times for Kurt to show up. "You could have called, given me some warning."

Kurt struck an arrogant pose and winked. "What? Are you too busy in this burg to have time for a colleague and very close friend?"

She blushed at the suggestive smirk that appeared

on Kurt's face. He was deliberately taunting Noah. "I am busy, as a matter of fact."

"I only need a few minutes, then I'll be on my way." He faced Noah. "But I need to talk to you alone."

Noah shifted slightly toward her. "Do you want me to stay?"

She rested one hand in the center of his chest, surprised at how hard his heart was beating. He was genuinely worried about her. The thought softened her anxiety and gave her great comfort. "I'll be fine. I'll see you tomorrow."

Noah gave Kurt a hard stare, then placed a light kiss on her lips as if staking his claim before guiding her to the door. "I'll call you later."

She nodded, waiting until she saw him go down the steps and outside before closing the apartment door and touching her fingers to her mouth. He'd kissed her. Why? Had it been a warning to Kurt or merely a way to reassure her that he'd be there if she needed him. Her heart tightened. She wanted to believe he'd kissed her because he cared, but she had to be careful and not read too much into it. That would be foolish.

Right now she had to deal with Kurt.

Beth stepped into the kitchen to see Kurt drinking from Noah's coffee mug. Irked to the limit, she took the mug away, dumped out the liquid and faced him.

"Who was that guy? A local farmer?"

His snobbish attitude rankled. "He happens to be a structural engineer."

"Really?" He glanced around her rooms. "So how can you stand to live here? I mean, this apartment is huge, but this town is off the grid. Nice tree."

He pointed to the pencil-thin Christmas tree she'd

put up. She really didn't care what he thought. "I'm actually very happy here. I like being home again."

"Well, you won't be happy here for long. I guess you heard about the shake-up in the company? Noreen taking charge and all that. So I'm out, and I couldn't be happier. I'm starting my own dance troupe. I've been offered the artistic director's job with Dance Unique. They have new backers who plan on turning it into a first-class company, and they've given me carte blanche to hire the personnel. I want you to come on board as the choreographer. Your name alone will shoot us to the top."

The offer was too good to be true. "Kurt, I appreciate you thinking of me, but I'm not nearly ready to go back to dancing full-time, and classical ballet is probably over for good."

"I know that, but hear me out. I think you'll be excited. There's only one hitch. I need an answer by Christmas."

Beth listened as Kurt outlined the details of his plan but made no promises. She breathed a sigh of relief when he finally left.

Curled up on her sofa, she thought through his offer, excitement building as she thought about the possibilities. She could reclaim her dream and the life she'd worked so hard for. The timing was perfect. By the time the new company was ready to perform, she'd be fully recovered. They would be focusing on other forms of dance and reaching out to young people. The idea was intriguing.

The money and the job security were enticing, too. An opportunity to create new ballets and new choreography was something she loved. She should have refused him immediately, but she told him she'd think it over. A month ago she would have jumped at the chance to leave Dover and go back to work in the dance world. Now she was hesitant. All because of Noah. Yet until she knew how Noah felt, she'd be smart to keep her options open, wouldn't she?

Beth grabbed a pillow and hugged it close. But hadn't she just decided to put her life in balance? Could she do that if she went back to New York? She'd started reading her Bible again and had even signed up for a women's bible study in the New Year.

She wanted to scream in confusion. Kurt's offer appealed to her ego. Why did God do this? She'd finally accepted that her dancing was over, she'd let it go and was turning her energies toward new dreams, then He dumps this big opportunity in her lap as if reminding her what her true dream was. What was she supposed to do? Was God saying don't let go? Was she walking away too soon? She'd been at peace with her decision, but now she was questioning that choice.

If only the Lord would give answers to her prayers in a loud voice, or write it across the sky. How were you supposed to know what God's will for your life was?

What she wanted was to talk it over with Noah, but she knew what he'd say. At the very least, she wanted to hear his voice. She'd told him she'd call. He was probably worried. Had he been protective because he was a gentleman and Kurt had posed a threat, or because he cared? He had kissed her before he left.

Her heart lodged in her throat as she waited for him to answer. She smiled when she heard his smooth voice. "Hi. It's me."

"Everything okay?"

"Yes. Kurt is obnoxious but harmless. I'm sorry he ruined our talk."

"Yeah. Well, I'm glad you're all right."

His casual response triggered concern. She'd expected him to bombard her with questions. Something in Noah's tone was off. "Are you all right? Is something wrong?"

A heavy sigh was her answer. "Yvonne called. She's coming in tomorrow to spend time with Chloe. She wants to see her in the *Christmas Dreams* show."

"Oh." No wonder he was distracted.

"I need to go. Can we talk tomorrow?"

"Yes, of course." She hung up, her mood sinking. She'd been hoping for a word of comfort from Noah, but now she longed to comfort him. She knew how worried he was for Chloe. With her mother showing up, so did the potential for another heartbreak for the little girl. That was far more important than her own silly problems.

Tonight her prayers would all be for Chloe, and that this time, Yvonne would stay true to her word.

Noah poured his fourth cup of coffee and spooned in sugar and a splash of creamer before returning to his desk. He didn't like working in the front office. The expanse of windows made him visible to everyone who passed by, which would be great if he was a merchant trying to sell goods. Not so much when he was promoting an engineering business. But right now, he needed to be visible, and an empty room said closed not open. Working out front had snagged his first private client, albeit a very difficult and frustrating one. Still, he'd be glad when he could land some commercial jobs, hire a receptionist and move his desk to the back room.

But that wasn't what had him sucking down caffeine like a student on an all-nighter.

He couldn't shake the image of Beth wrapped in the arms of the irritating Kurt. The man's possessive attitude still made his blood boil. He'd held Beth in his arms as if he had a right, and the smirk on his face begged to be wiped off with a fist. He'd only left because Beth had assured him she would be fine, but he'd been tormented by the man's remark about changing Beth's life. Had he come to lure her back to the dance? This made him wonder if there was more to their relationship. He knew what was eating at him. Jealousy. He had no right to feel that way, but there it was.

Unfortunately, by the time she'd called him to say she was okay, he'd barely listened. He'd been too distracted by the news of Yvonne's visit. Chloe had texted her mom the moment she'd learned of her starring role in the Christmas show, and her mother had responded in her usual way, promising their child that she would come to the performance, film it for her TV show, then take her to New Orleans for a long fun weekend.

He'd tried to prepare Chloe to be disappointed, but she wouldn't listen. She went up to her room and started to pack, leaving him dreading the huge letdown sure to come. Yvonne was due in town today. She planned to stay through the Christmas show tomorrow night, then she and Chloe were going down to New Orleans for a few days of shopping and to take in the Christmas events.

Please, Lord, don't let Yvonne let my little girl down again.

His ringtone drew his hand to his cell phone in his pocket. Gram. "Is she here?" He'd wanted to wait at the house, but he had a heavy load of inspections today and another go-round with Kramer at the old house.

"Yes. She picked Chloe up a few minutes ago. They're going up to Jackson to shop then have dinner at the Lady Banks Inn. Chloe is super excited."

"And Yvonne?" There was a long pause before his gram answered, putting a knot in his chest.

"Her usual busy self."

Noah rubbed his forehead. Translation—Yvonne was preoccupied with her cell phone and probably wouldn't spend much time actually talking to her daughter. "Did she seem happy to see Chloe?"

"She made a grand show on her arrival."

"I'm sure she did."

Gram tried to reassure him that everything would be fine before she hung up. He wanted to believe her, but he sent a few more pleas heavenward just in case. Leaning back in his chair, he rubbed his bottom lip, trying to quell the churning in his gut. He pulled the key ring from his pocket and studied it. He'd wanted to talk to Beth last night about the words she'd put on the back. But Kurt had interrupted them, and now Yvonne was intruding, as well.

Light tapping on his door pulled his attention away. Beth pushed it open, her hazel eyes narrowed in concern.

"Are you okay?"

Quickly he shoved the key ring into his pocket. Now was not the time to discuss it. "Yeah. As good as I can be, I guess."

"Did she come?"

"Yes. They're going up to one of the malls in Jackson to shop."

Beth moved closer, biting her bottom lip. "I hate to ask this, but will Chloe be safe with her?"

Her concern for his child touched him deeply. He took her hand in his, squeezing it gently. "Yes. Yvonne would never do anything to hurt her child. In her own way, she loves Chloe." His words did little to ease the troubled frown on Beth's face. "Don't worry. She won't try to kidnap her. That would interfere with her glamorous life. She's not going to go off and forget about her, and if something does come up, she'll bring her home. It's not Chloe's physical well-being I'm worried about. It's her mental state."

"She wants her mom to love her."

"I don't know how many more times she can be shoved aside and rejected."

"She's a hopeful little girl. She believes in the goodness of others. But I worry, too. Then I remember that she has you, and I know she'll be all right. I think her security in your love allows her to maintain her hope that her mom will change."

"Thank you. I needed to hear that. I feel pretty inadequate at times. I don't know much about little girls. I'd be totally lost without Gram."

"Noah, I adore Chloe. If there's ever anything I can do, please don't hesitate to ask. I was a girl once, you know."

He remembered. Vividly. "So you were." Their gazes meshed, setting off tiny sparks along his skin. The image of Kurt holding Beth flashed across his mind, forcing him to retreat. "So, what did your friend have for you that will change your life?"

She looked down, hooking a strand of hair behind her ear. A sure sign she was reluctant to share.

"He had a job offer."

Noah's heart chilled, releasing all the old fears and hurts. "I see. So when do you leave?"

"I haven't given him an answer yet. He needs to know by Christmas."

He wanted to fight to convince her to stay, but like Chloe, he'd come to realize he couldn't make others behave the way he wanted. "You do what you think best. I want you to be happy." He shuffled the papers on his desk, surprised to find he really meant what he said. "I need to get to work."

Her eyes were wide and slightly moist as she nodded and turned to leave. "I have to get back. The phone is ringing. Will you let me know how Chloe is if you hear from her?"

"Sure, but I don't expect to. She'll be too busy to think of her old dad."

"Shopping will do that to you. Pushes everything else out of your mind."

"If you say so."

As soon as Beth left, Noah gathered up his work orders for the day, slipped them into his leather folder then went out the back door to his car. He'd told Beth the truth when he said Yvonne would take good care of Chloe, but he never could completely let go of his concern. Work was a good diversion, provided he could concentrate long enough to get the job done. He hated having to share his child. Even with her mother.

But for some reason, he didn't mind sharing her with Beth.

Chapter Ten

Beth took her time walking back to her apartment
Friday night, enjoying the glow of the lights. She'd
met Jen at the Magnolia Café for a meal and a little
girl time. They'd ironed out a few details for the show
the next day and spent the rest of the time catching up.
There was never time to talk at rehearsals, and they
were both eager to restore their friendship. The longer
Beth remained in Dover, the more settled and secure
she felt. But she couldn't totally dismiss the opportunity Kurt had offered. She'd prayed about it, but still
had no clear answer.

If things between her and Noah were different, her
choice would be so much easier. But at the moment,
she had no idea where their relationship stood. She
knew he cared for her, but to what extent? One minute he was placing kisses on her lips, the next he was
pulling away.

Kurt's offer was to blame for part of that. She had
to make that decision before she could move forward,
but her emotions were tilting up and down between
the choices like a child's seesaw. Her desire to dance

was still strong, but so was her growing contentment here in Dover.

Pulling her keys from her purse, she stepped into the recessed entry of her building. Movement in the shadows stole her breath. She froze, her heart pounding.

"Miss Beth."

As her eyes adjusted to the low light, she saw Chloe seated on the floor, her back to the apartment door, her knees drawn up to her chest. Fear for her own safety shifted to fear for the little girl. "Chloe, sweetie, what are you doing here?"

"Waiting for you."

Beth opened her arms, and the little girl scrambled to her feet and into her embrace. "Chloe, what happened?"

Her little hands were chilly despite the thick jacket she wore, and Beth held her closer as she began to cry. She noticed the small rolling suitcase beside her.

Quickly, Beth hurried her upstairs to the apartment and settled her at the table. "I'm going to make you some hot chocolate, and then you can tell me what happened."

"She had to go back."

Beth slid into the chair, taking Chloe's hand in hers. "Your mom?"

Chloe nodded, wiping fresh tears from her cheeks. "She got a call when we were at the mall, and she was mad that she had to bring me all the way back here."

Beth clenched her teeth to prevent herself from voicing her anger. "Why here? Why didn't she take you home?"

Chloe's blue eyes glanced downward. "I told her

Dad and Gram were at a meeting and weren't home. I told her you were."

"And she just dropped you off without making sure I was home?" Beth struggled to understand that level of irresponsibility.

"I told her I had a key 'cause you were my teacher."

"Oh, Chloe. Why didn't you want to go home?"

"'Cause my dad would be all mad and stuff. He never wants me to go with Mom. She was going to film the *Christmas Dreams* musical, and interview me for her TV show, and then we were supposed to go to New Orleans." Tears rolled down her cheeks. Her mouth puckered into a pitiful frown.

"I'm so sorry." She held her close a moment before retrieving the hot chocolate from the microwave and urging Chloe toward the sofa. After settling her in under the fleece throw, she gave her the mug. "I need to call your dad."

"No. Please don't. I don't want to go home. I want to stay here with you."

"Chloe, he'll be worried. Won't your mom call him and tell him she had to leave?"

The guilty look appeared again.

"I told her he had his phone off, and it wouldn't be on until late because of his meeting."

"Oh, Chloe, I know this is hard for you, but I have to call him. He loves you, and he'll be frantic."

"Okay, but please can I stay here with you? I can't talk to him about Mom, and I can talk to you. Please don't make me leave."

Beth paused with her cell in her hand, torn between the pitiful pleas coming from the little girl and her responsibility as an adult. "Chloe, I have to call him, but

I'll see if he will let you spend the night with me. We can talk all night if you want, but tomorrow is the big show. You need to get some sleep so you'll be ready for the *Nutcracker* number."

"I promise I'll sleep and then go home in the morning."

Beth stepped into the bedroom to make her call, bracing herself for Noah's shock and anger. She wasn't disappointed. He was furious.

"I knew agreeing to this weekend was a mistake. I try not to get too involved because Chloe loves her mother. But this is the last straw. I'll be right over to get her."

"No. I think you should let her stay here with me tonight. She wants to talk, and since I'm a neutral party it'll be easier for her to open up to me. We've become close, and the fact that she asked her mom to bring her to me tells me she trusts me." The silence bothered her. Would he refuse?

"Yeah. You may be right. Let me know what happens, okay? And, Beth, tell her I love her."

Her heart warmed at the tenderness in his voice. "Of course. I told her you'd come get her first thing. Tomorrow is going to be a busy day so we both need our sleep, and we need to get to the theater early."

"Beth, thank you. I'm sorry she was dumped on your doorstep, but I'm grateful you were there to take care of her. I appreciate what you're doing. I'll make it up to you somehow."

"I adore Chloe, Noah. And all I need is for you to be my friend again, and trust me when I say that I won't hurt Chloe."

"I know. Beth, when the show is over we need to talk. I found the key chain, and I read what it said."

"Oh."

"I think there are things we should have said to each other a long time ago."

What did he mean? Was he going to remind her that he hadn't cared then, and he still didn't? That was something she'd think about later. Right now Chloe was her first concern.

Her little roommate was standing at the French doors leading to the balcony when she returned to the living room. She went to her, draped her arms over the slender shoulders and held her close. "The lights are beautiful, aren't they?"

Chloe nodded. "I wanted my mom to see them."

The wistful tone in her voice dragged Beth's heart down to her stomach. "I'm sorry, Chloe. I know you're disappointed."

"Why does my mom like her job better than me?"

Beth turned the little girl around and hugged her. "Oh, sweetie, I don't think she does. But I think she's so happy in her job that she forgets what's important."

"How can she forget me? I never forget her."

Beth steered the child to the sofa and pulled her down beside her, covering them both with the soft throw. She picked up the remote that controlled the lights and switched them off, leaving only the glow of the Christmas lights outside to illuminate the room. Sometimes it was easier to talk in the dark.

She hugged Chloe to her side while she gathered her thoughts. "I don't know your mother, so I don't know what her reasons are or what she dreams about. But I do know that some people are good at loving and some aren't. And some people have big dreams they work very hard to achieve. It becomes the most important thing in their life, and they'll do whatever it takes to make that dream come true."

"Like your dream to be a ballerina?"

The simple question pricked her conscience. "Yes. I worked hard and my dream came true, but I had to give up a lot of things along the way. Like friends and vacations and a lot of other things that at the time didn't seem as important as learning to be a better dancer and practicing to stay in shape. I even forgot about my family along the way."

"You forgot Miss Francie?"

"I didn't forget who she was, but I forgot to call her. I forgot her birthday. I forgot to come home to visit, and that made her sad."

"Do you think my mom's dream is to be on TV?"

"Maybe right now. Your mom is trying to be a success, and along the way she's forgetting what's important. The sad part is one day she'll realize she missed all these adventures with you, but it'll be too late. You'll be all grown up and maybe even have a little girl of your own. But I'm sure she loves you. I loved my mom even though I didn't think about her much. I just lost track of the priorities."

"Maybe I should call her and tell her how much fun we could have."

"You could."

Chloe snuggled closer. "But it wouldn't matter, would it? She always breaks her promises. Daddy tells me not to count on her when she promises things, but I want them to come true so much."

"Of course you do."

"Miss Beth, do you think God would be mad if I stopped loving my mom?"

Beth rested her head on Chloe's, feeling her pain as if it was her own. "I think He might. He doesn't stop loving you just because you make a mistake. But maybe you could look at this in a more grown-up way. Sooner or later, everyone lets us down. A mom, a job, a friend. God is the only one who never fails us. The next time your mom sets up a visit, be excited, be happy, but hold a little caution in your mind, too. Maybe you won't be so disappointed then."

"I guess my mom won't ever be the way I wish she was."

"I don't know. Maybe someday. But for now, you concentrate on the oodles of good things in your life. Your gram, your dad who adores you and your friends. You can have plenty of adventures with them."

"And you, too?"

"Of course. We're having a huge adventure with the Christmas show."

"I wish you were my mom, Miss Beth. We'd have way cool adventures together."

She blinked away sudden tears. "Thank you, Chloe. That's the nicest thing anyone has ever said to me. I'm glad we're friends. And I'm glad you came here tonight. I want you to make me a promise, though. You need to talk to your dad about tonight and what happened with your mother."

"Okay, but he'll say the same old thing. 'Don't get your hopes up when your mother calls.'"

"Will you the next time?"

Chloe sighed. "No. She might be good on TV, but she's not very good at being a mom."

"But your dad is very good at being your father, don't you agree?"

"He's the most phantasmagorical dad ever." She grinned. "And he's handsome, too, don't you think?"

"I wouldn't know about that. We'd better get to bed, or you'll be the Clara that falls asleep and never wakes up for her dance."

Tucked in bed with Chloe sound asleep beside her, Beth's thoughts went to Noah. He was a fantastic father and a disturbingly handsome man. But it was his heart she'd fallen in love with all those years ago, and his heart had captured hers again.

It's why she'd engraved her feelings on the back of the key chain. She'd been too shy and insecure to say the words back then. But now he'd read them, and he wanted to talk. Why?

She wanted to believe what her eyes and her senses were telling her whenever she and Noah were together. She wanted to believe the light in his eyes was for her, the tender smile for her and the gentle touches for her.

In that moment she realized that Noah was her new dream. Noah and Chloe and a future together.

But what if she was wrong?

Nothing, not even her most triumphant role with the Forsythe Company, came close to the elation coursing through her tonight. The cast was taking its third curtain call. The audience was on their feet. The little theater's production of *Christmas Dreams* had gone on without a hitch. Her dancers hadn't missed a step. Her heart was so full, she wasn't sure she could contain her joy.

Jen came to her side and gave her a quick hug. "We did it. I can't believe how well it all went."

Beth glanced at the crowd, only now starting to leave as the cast made their way off the stage. The shouts of joy and laughter filled the old building. Cast members hugged one another and shared high fives. The children ran to greet proud parents, who were waiting to congratulate them.

"Miss Beth."

She saw her three students hurrying toward her, their flouncing costumes rustling as they came.

Hannah grinned up at her as she tugged the bow from her hair. "We didn't forget a step."

Abby laughed. "You almost messed up on that turn."

"Almost."

Chloe slipped her hand into Beth's. "We got lots of applause."

"That's because you were so adorable. I'm so proud of you girls. Of everyone."

Chloe hugged her, which drew the other two into a group hug. "We love you, Miss Beth."

Abby nodded. "I'm glad you're my aunt. This was so cool."

Hannah nodded. "Can we do this again?"

Noah came to her side. "You might have to. Judging by the response, once word spreads about how awesome the show was, you might have to give another performance."

He opened his arms and gave Chloe a big hug.

"Did you like me, Daddy?"

"You danced liked a professional. You were beautiful. I was very proud." He handed her a small bouquet of white miniature roses. "These are for you."

Gram joined the group. "My little princess. You were amazing." She smiled at the others. "Y'all stole the show."

Hannah spotted her mom and darted off with a wave. Abby spun around when her dad called her name and hurried to join him and her mom.

Beth looked at Noah. He was looking at her with such warmth and tenderness she couldn't breathe.

"Thank you. I know I've had my concerns about Chloe getting caught up in this dance thing, but I've never seen her so happy. She really loves to dance. You are a very good teacher."

"It's easy when the students are so eager."

Gram took Chloe's hand. "Let's get you out of that costume, and then we'll go celebrate."

Gram had arranged a wrap party at the senior center for all the cast and crew.

Noah turned to Beth. "You're coming to the party, aren't you?"

She wanted nothing more than to extend this night as long as possible. She did want to celebrate. With him. "Of course."

"You two go on. We'll meet you there."

"Guess that's our cue to leave." Noah touched her arm lightly. "Would you rather walk or drive?"

"Let's walk. I want to savor this feeling and stroll through the lights of town."

Outside they took their time along the sidewalk, crossing to the park. The town was filled with visitors, making it hard to stay close. Noah took her hand. The lights were on in Dover, creating the sensation of walking inside a lovely snow globe. Without the snow, of course. "(There's No Place Like) Home for the Holidays" filled the air, elevating her good mood up another level.

The atmosphere was electric with lingering excitement. Everywhere they turned, people were talking about the show. Three times on their walk across the park, Beth was stopped and congratulated on the event. By the time they entered the senior center, Beth's heart was soaring.

Evelyn and Chloe were already there. Gram hushed the crowd and came forward, motioning her and Jen to her side. "We contemplated several ways to thank you for your hard work and dedication. We had a long list of gifts we could purchase to express our appreciation. In the end we realized nothing we could buy could truly demonstrate the depth of gratitude we feel. So we're giving you our hearts instead. Thank you. Both."

The three Claras stepped forward and handed each woman—Evelyn, Jen and herself—a large bouquet of roses. Beth's vision was blurred with tears, but she could see hers were pink. Her favorite and exactly like the ones her father always had given her after a performance. That had to be Noah's doing.

The applause was peppered with shouts for a speech. Jen said a few words. Beth tried to remember all the people who'd helped, but her emotions were so close to the surface she gave up, muttering a soft thank-you before hugging the flowers close and thanking the Lord for this blessing she'd never expected.

Noah watched from the sidelines as Jen and Beth each gave a short speech of appreciation. Beth glanced over her shoulder in his direction when she spoke of the talented painters and carpenters who had added so much to the production.

Noah leaned against a post, watching his girls enjoy the wrap party. Gram was in her element, accepting the adoration and gratitude of the cast and crew. Chloe was laughing, huddled with her friends, giggling and screeching in happiness.

His Beth was glowing from the triumph of the production. Her smile lit up the room, making her eyes sparkle. She glided around the room, speaking to everyone with gracious sincerity. Many times he saw her tug Chloe to her side and speak to her. His chest expanded with happiness, threatening to crack his ribs from the pressure.

When the party began to wind down, Gram came over to collect Chloe. "Are you coming?"

"Shortly. My truck is still at the theater, and I want to make sure Beth gets home safely. It's late."

Gram patted his arm in approval, a knowing smile brightening her eyes.

Beth gave his daughter and Gram a hug, then looked in his direction. His heart warmed ten degrees at the affection in her hazel eyes. As she came toward him, he couldn't help but admire her grace and the way her red dress swished around her knees. She was the most beautiful woman he'd ever known. There was a sweetness about her that drew him to her, made him want to keep her close to his side and never let her go.

He looked into her eyes and saw that her exhilaration had given way to fatigue. She'd worked hard on the *Christmas Dreams* show. She needed a few days to rest and recharge.

"You ready to go?"

"Yes. I've suddenly lost all my energy."

"Then I'd better walk you home to make sure you don't fall asleep on your feet." He draped her fringed shawl over her shoulders, noticing that the little sparkles woven in the threads matched the sparkle in her eyes. Outside, the glory lights were still on downtown, flooding every nook and cranny of the square in a soft, dreamy glow. The crowds had thinned, and they took their time walking home.

"I want to add my congratulations to all the others. The show was amazing. You and Jen deserve all the praise."

"I don't know about that. We didn't do it alone, you know. Besides, like I stressed to my dancers, this was for Him. He's the one who came to earth."

"Point taken. Nevertheless, I'm proud of you and I'm glad you asked Chloe to be in the show. She's beyond happy."

"I'm so glad. She appears to have bounced back from last night."

"I think so." He took her hand. "I can't thank you enough for taking care of her. I'm just sorry she didn't feel she could come to me when her mom had to leave."

"She was angry and confused, and I think all she wanted was to talk to someone."

"She could have talked to me."

"Normally, but you would have been so furious at her mother, you might not have listened to Chloe."

He had to admit she had a point. He would have exploded. "I called her mother, and there's going to be some changes made. I can't put Chloe through this again. I just hope she understands."

"I believe she will. I think she finally realized that

she can't make her mother change to fit her wishes. I tried to explain about dreams, and how easy it is to lose track of the important things in life. I think she understood some of it, and hopefully she'll be more cautious the next time her mother calls."

"It's hard being forgotten by people who are supposed to care. You feel like you don't matter." He saw her wince, only then realizing how she might have taken his statement. It hadn't been directed at her. He pulled her a little closer. "I'm glad she had you to talk to. That she trusted you with her feelings."

"I'll always be there for her. I'm afraid your daughter has stolen my heart." Stepping into the shadows of the entryway, she smiled into his eyes. "Thanks for walking me home."

"Speaking of hearts, we need to talk."

Even in the dim light he could see the worry darken her eyes. "All right. We can go upstairs if you'd like."

He thought about the cozy atmosphere in her apartment, the sense of home he'd experienced there. Being alone with her while feeling the way he did wasn't a good idea. "No. That's playing with fire. This will do fine." He slipped his hand into his pocket and pulled out the key chain. "I want to know what you meant. 'Every time you touch this you will be touching my heart. Love, Beth.'"

She tugged her shawl closer, avoiding his eyes. "Noah."

"Did you mean it?" His heart thudded fiercely in his chest. He searched her face, longing to hear confirmation of his suspicions.

"Yes. At the time, I had a huge crush on you."

A crush? Not what he'd hoped to hear, but it was a

start and he pushed ahead. "What about now?" That's what he had to know.

"What do you mean?"

"How do you feel about me now?" She took so long to respond, his throat tightened. He was fearful of having misread all the signals and the sparks between them. She met his gaze, the connection melting them together as if they physically touched. Her hand came up to rest on his cheek.

"I think my crush never faded."

Pulse racing, he pulled her into his arms and kissed her with all the stored-up emotion he'd carried for years. He wanted her to have no doubts about his feelings. She slipped her arms around his neck, burrowing her fingers into his hair and sending his mind spinning. Kissing her was everything he'd dreamed of, and it filled him with a sense of home. For the first time since losing his parents, his heart was whole again.

He ended the kiss, holding her against his chest, inhaling the sweet floral scent while his chin rested on her silky hair. He trailed his fingers through the strands along her temple. "If I'd read this inscription that day, everything would have been different."

"Would it?" Her words were muffled against his chest.

"Yes, because I would have given you my gift even if it wasn't wrapped."

"You never told me what it was."

"A promise ring. I wanted you to be connected to me while I was at college. I wanted you to know how I felt."

"How did you feel? I was never sure."

"I was in love with you. I had been from the first

day, but I didn't figure I had a chance. Not against your passion for dance."

"I guess we were both too afraid to admit what we were feeling. So what now?" She slid her arms around his waist. "This thing between us, where do we go from here?"

He held her closer, finding a peace in her closeness he'd never experienced before. "Take our time. See what happens. It's not just my heart involved now. I have Chloe to think about, too."

"You know I would never hurt her."

"I know." He tilted her face upward and kissed her again, overcome by a longing to never let her go. When he broke the kiss, he gulped in air and stepped back. "You'd better go on up."

She touched his cheek. "Good night, Noah. Think of me tonight."

"I always do."

He forced himself to turn and walk away, but stopped at the edge of the entryway. "Beth, if I'd told you how I felt that day, would you have stayed?" He wasn't sure why he'd asked the question and wasn't at all sure he wanted to hear the answer.

She held his gaze a long moment, then shook her head. "No. I would have chosen to dance. I didn't understand what I was giving up. I won't make that mistake again."

It wasn't the answer he'd hoped for, but it was one that gave him hope. And for now that was enough.

Chapter Eleven

Beth snuggled deeper into the covers, reliving Noah's kiss once again. She'd gone straight to bed, not wanting anything to diminish the feeling of euphoria and bliss still lingering in her senses. The tenderness in his kiss and the gentle way he'd held her had carried her away on emotions she'd never imagined. In his arms she found the sense of belonging she'd always craved.

She recalled again the sweet sensation of his kiss. So much had been revealed in that kiss.

Neither of them had declared their feelings outright, but the kiss had sent their relationship in a new direction—one she was eager to pursue. Was it possible to have a future with Noah? Could they move beyond the mistakes of the past and find a future together here in Dover? She prayed that was true because Noah was the only one she wanted to share her life with. The only one who knew her faults and her failings, and loved her in spite of them. He was her perfect partner.

Bright sunlight woke her the next morning. She'd overslept but got up feeling happier than she had in a long time. Her dreams had been filled with images of her and Noah dancing together, around and around, holding each other close, lost in their happiness.

She poured another cup of coffee and curled up on the sofa. For the moment it was still a dream. She had things to do today. Her first order of business was to call Kurt and tell him she wasn't interested. She wasn't sure why she'd taken so long to decide. The more she'd considered his offer, the more the truth had risen to the surface.

The thought of returning to a full-time dance career, with the constant stress and pressure, had brought a knot of tension into her chest. Since coming home she'd been sleeping better, eating better, even to the point of needing new clothes. She greeted each morning eager to start the day.

Looking back, she could see her passion for ballet had started to wane long before the failed romance and the miscarriage. She'd just been too committed to realize it. She'd had her time in the spotlight and she'd lived every aspect of her dream.

Kurt had said she wouldn't be happy here for long. But he was wrong. She wanted different things now. A line from one of her favorite show tunes came to mind: "The gift was ours to borrow." She'd been given the gift of dance and had used it to the fullness of her ability. Now it was time to let someone else use their gift.

And she would explore a new gift and a new direction. She placed the call to Kurt, who did his best to change her mind, but in the end he was surprisingly supportive.

Relieved and buoyed with anticipation, she opened her laptop, logged on to the local MLS and pulled up the commercial listings, searching for a place to open her dance school. She wouldn't tell Noah just yet. She'd wait until it was all settled. That way he'd know for certain she was staying in Dover, and he could depend on her not to run off again.

Financially she was in pretty good shape. She'd been so busy working that she'd spent very little of her earnings, and money went a lot further in Dover than in New York.

She scrolled through the handful of properties, stopping on several possibilities. There was plenty of rental space available, but she preferred to own. A small knot formed in her stomach. Becoming a business owner was a big step. She had no idea what was involved in starting a dance school, or the necessary legalities. Would she need to be certified? Bonded? It wasn't simply a matter of getting a loan; there was also marketing and advertising to think about. The thought set her mind spinning. She pursed her lips and leaned back on the sofa.

Was she ready? Was she capable? All she'd ever known was dancing, and a large part of that consisted of other people telling her what to do—how to stand, hold her head, position her arms, feet, hips, neck.

She forced the negative thoughts away. She was getting ahead of herself. First she had to find a suitable place. Then she could take her time working out the rest.

Her gaze landed on the address of a familiar building. Miss Barker's School of Dance. Her old teacher. She'd taken lessons there three times a week until she'd started private lessons in Jackson. The picture showed a very old, run-down structure. Was this a sign? A nudge from on high that she could step in and restore the school? She searched the screen for the owner and saw that the property was represented by a local bank.

Logically, she should work with her mom on this purchase, but she wasn't ready to share her plans. She wanted to prove to her family and herself that she could take charge of her life, and go in a new direction. But if she mentioned her idea to the family, she'd be buried in advice and far too many helpful good intentions. She knew how quickly a plan like this could fall apart. She'd already had one career dream crumble. She wasn't eager to lose another one. Once things were finalized, she'd make the announcement.

Tiny fingers of doubt crept along her nerves. Was she a fool to consider opening a dance school? She thought of her three little ballerinas, and the ladies at the senior center. No. Dover needed a place for children to learn to appreciate the dance, and a teacher who would make sure they were taught modest moves.

What would Noah think? Would starting a business in Dover finally assure him she wasn't going back to the stage?

That was her prayer, because if it didn't, then she had no hope of ever convincing him.

Noah pulled his truck to a stop in front of Kramer's dilapidated old house, his mood sagging when he recognized the owner's vehicle sitting near the back. Kramer had asked him to come by and check out a few structural issues he'd uncovered during demolition. This was the last place Noah wanted to be this morning. His thoughts were still bouncing back to last night and the kiss he'd shared with Beth.

He didn't put much trust in dreams, but last night,

holding Beth, he'd seen his old dream reforming in front of him. A wife, a family and a home of his own. His dream was giving Chloe the kind of security and completeness he'd known, but lost.

They'd both danced around actually admitting they loved each other. She'd said her crush was still there; he'd confessed to loving her in the past. But they'd agreed to explore their feelings. That was a long way from the timid, insecure kids they'd been long ago.

Yet part of him remained wary. There was a lot of scar tissue to deal with.

"Carlisle."

Noah glanced up to see Kramer waving at him. He climbed out of the truck and joined him. His first client was proving to be more trouble than he was worth. Noah had thought about walking away, but the guy was the type to make his displeasure known to anyone who would listen, and bad word-of-mouth could kill his business before it even got off the ground.

"Glad you're here. I need you to look at this floor and tell me why it's sloping."

Noah followed him inside to the back of the house, but stopped before they entered the old kitchen. The wall that had separated the rooms had been removed. A closer look revealed that another wall had been torn down, too, and a quick glance upward triggered his alarm. "When did you take these walls down?"

"A few days ago. I need to get some of this work done if I'm going to make any money on this flip."

The statement unleashed a flare of anger in Noah. Kramer was trying to take a beautiful old home filled with fine craftsmanship and turn it into an open-concept hollow shell. But that wasn't his concern. "You should have checked with me first. You've taken down a load-bearing wall. Didn't your carpenter know that?"

"I didn't ask him. I did this myself to save some change."

Noah gritted his teeth. "That second floor is already sagging." He pointed to the obviously bowed joist above them. "You'd better shore that up before the entire second level falls down." He glanced around the space for something to shore up the beam, but could only find two-by-fours, which were not nearly strong enough to support the weight.

"I'll do that, but first look at this floor." He walked into the kitchen area and bounced up and down. The floor beneath his feet moved. "What's going on?"

Noah stooped down. The boards were clearly soft and probably rotten, but it was the supports beneath that concerned him. "Not sure until I can pull up some of the boards and get a look at the foundation."

Kramer grunted. "Great. I can't afford any more major hits. Are you sure about this?"

"Like I said, I'll have to get under the house, but it's a safe guess that either your joists aren't large enough or they're rotted out. It could also mean your piers have sunk into the ground."

"Meaning what?"

"A new foundation. We'd have to pour a concrete pad, set a new pier and put in stronger joists. Then beef up the floors, and maybe add metal leveling supports and stabilize the house from sinking into the ground more."

"Can you get under there now?"

"Not today. But I'll come back tomorrow and take a look. In the meantime, you need to get this ceiling stabilized. If you want this whole space open, you're going to need an I beam."

"You said a fifteen-foot beam would be plenty strong enough."

"That's when you were only removing one wall."

"Look, can't we work something out? Do we really need to be so picky? I mean, you're a building inspector, too, aren't you?"

Noah kept a tight hold on his anger. "Yes, but since you've hired me as your engineer, I won't be doing the city inspection on this house. We have building codes for a reason, Mr. Kramer, and if you want to continue to remodel this house, you'll have to meet them." He glanced at his phone. "I have another appointment. I'll try to get back out here tomorrow to look under the house. In the meantime—" he pointed to the sagging ceiling "—get that shored up."

Kramer's rude comment hung in the air as Noah walked away. He couldn't wait for this job to be finished. It wasn't the first time he'd been asked to let something slide to hold down costs, but he wasn't going to pass on something that could fail down the road. It was his responsibility to make sure structures were safe and compliant with current codes. If something he signed off on failed, then he would be held responsible.

Beth gripped the phone tighter in her palm as a violent wave of heat coursed through her veins, and blood pounded in her ears. Her hopeful excitement when she'd seen the name of the bank on an incoming email had deflated like a punctured tire when she'd read that the inspection had failed and she couldn't move forward with her application. She'd immediately placed a call to the loan officer, Burt Valens. "What do I have to do now?"

"I'm afraid there's nothing to be done on that property. The inspector recommended the building be condemned. It's not safe."

"But can't it be fixed? Restored or whatever?"

"I'm afraid not. Mr. Carlisle reported the structure was too far gone to redeem. I suggest you select another property. We'd be happy to process your application at that time."

"Thank you." Beth could barely speak around the anger clogging her throat. Noah. He'd done the inspection on her building and condemned it. The place looked rough. She knew it would need fixing up before she could open her studio; that's why she'd asked for an inspection. But condemned? No way.

She set her jaw. This had nothing to do with the condition of that building. This was about Noah's stubborn refusal to believe she wasn't going to suddenly walk out of his life. He didn't trust her, and this was his way of getting back at her. He was making her pay for something his ex-wife had done.

Glancing over at his office, she saw him moving around. Time to have a long overdue talk. Striding across the entryway, she yanked open his office door. He spun and looked at her, his dark brows pulled down into a fierce frown.

"Why did you do that?"

He swallowed. "Do what?"

"Condemn my building? I can't believe you'd carry a grudge this far. How dare you deliberately sabotage my future that way?"

Noah held up his hand and came toward her. "Hold it right there. I have no idea what you're talking about."

"Miss Barker's old building on Liberty Street. Your inspection caused me to lose a loan from the bank."

"You're the potential buyer? Why? What do you want with that run-down place?"

She wasn't ready to tell him that. "That's not important. You deliberately condemned that building."

"Beth, that building isn't safe. My report was based on facts and a thorough inspection. The place is ready to fall down. Besides, I had no idea you were the one wanting the inspection."

"I don't believe you. I'm positive my name was on the work order. You are determined to make me pay for leaving."

"No, I'd never do that. You know me better than that."

"I thought I did, but now I realize I don't know you at all." Furious, she whirled around and stormed back to her office, too upset to think clearly. Noah followed behind, clearly determined to explain himself.

"Beth, I want to know what's going on. You owe me an explanation."

"Don't put this on me." She crossed her arms over her chest, breathing rapidly. "You're afraid. You've built this steel wall around your heart so you won't have to risk getting hurt again. You use me and Chloe and anything else you can think of to keep yourself protected. I thought I saw that wall coming down and you opening up. Until Chloe's mother messed up and Kurt appeared, and now you're diving behind that wall again and shutting everyone out."

"You're wrong."

"You forget who you're talking to, Noah. I know you better than anyone. I know what you're most afraid of. I know how much you want a family again. A place to belong. Just like I do." With some of her anger spent, she took a deep breath and met his gaze. "We found that place in each other, but we were too young and naive to understand what we had. We were the right people. It was just the wrong time."

Noah ran a hand through his hair before resting his hands on his hips. "I didn't do this to hurt you. I didn't even know you were the one trying to buy the place."

"Then change your report."

"I can't do that. The building is too dangerous. I won't say it's safe when it's not just to make you happy."

Noah rubbed his forehead, then lowered his head and stared at the desk. Beth waited for him to continue. His shoulders braced. He reached over and picked up the printed boarding pass lying on the desk. His jaw flexed rapidly as he read the destination. "New York?"

His eyes were the color of an angry summer sky. She hastened to explain. "Yes, I'm going to—"

He waved the paper at her. "Your friend's offer was too good to pass up."

"No. That's not why I'm going."

"But you are going."

"Yes, but if you let me explain—"

The door swished open and her mother hurried in. "Beth, I need that list of properties for the Andersons. I forgot to put it in my phone before I left. Hello, Noah."

"Francie." He sent a glare at Beth, tossed the paper back onto the desk then walked out, leaving a heavy tension in the air.

"Did I interrupt something?" Her mother cast a puzzled look in her direction. "What's wrong?"

Beth could barely speak around the pain and hurt clawing at her throat. "Noah condemned my building. And then he saw my boarding pass for New York." She sank into the desk chair, wiping tears from her eyes. "He thinks I'm walking away again."

Francie frowned. "You're leaving?"

"Yes, but I'll be right back. I'm due for a follow-up visit with my doctor in New York, and I decided to go right away and get it over with. Noah stormed out before I could explain, and I'm sure in his stubborn, distrustful way, he thinks I'm going back to work."

"And this building thing. What's that about?"

"Oh." Her guilty conscience swelled. "I was going to wait to tell you until it was all finalized, but I put an offer in on Miss Barker's old building, the one where I took lessons. It's for sale, and I thought it would be a good place to open my school." She shrugged. "Sort of carry on in her honor."

Her mother nodded. "You want to open a dance school. Here in Dover? I thought that was the very last thing you wanted to do."

She nodded. "It was, until I started teaching the girls and working with the seniors and helping with the show. Now it sounds like a good idea."

"I think so, too."

"But Noah did the inspection on the building and recommended it be condemned."

"Good for him."

"Whose side are you on?"

"His, in this case. Honey, I know that building. The owner lives in New England someplace, and he has no intention of fixing it up. He's only interested in the ground it sits on. How had you planned on paying for it? You sold the land your father gave you when you moved to New York."

"I know, and I don't regret it. But I'm in good shape financially. I can afford to do this."

"Why didn't you come to me about this?"

The hurt tone in her mother's voice scratched across her conscience. She should have thought things through better. "I wanted to accomplish it on my own, to prove to everyone I'd changed."

"I admire your intentions, but if you'd told me, I could have saved you a lot of trouble. If you really want to open a studio, I have several places better suited that wouldn't need much to get them ready. Or you could rent a place until you get up and running."

"I'd rather own."

"Okay. Scoot over."

Her mother pulled up another chair to the desk and quickly pulled up three locations on the computer. Beth took one look at the two-story property, with its blue paint and dark blue awnings, and knew it was perfect. "That's the one. Do you think I can afford it?"

"We'll make sure of it." She hit the print button and pulled the sheet from the printer.

"When do you go to New York?"

"Now. I need to leave for the airport in a few minutes. I have an appointment first thing tomorrow morning. I had just printed out my boarding pass when the bank called and I found out Noah had done the inspection on my building and condemned it. I accused him of doing it deliberately to hurt me."

Her mother frowned, studying her closely. "Do you

really think Noah would be so vindictive? Not to mention unethical."

With her shock and anger fading, Beth realized she'd overreacted. "No. He's too honorable to ever do something like that. I was upset. I guess I was lashing out at him without thinking."

"Maybe you'd better go explain things to him."

"No. I think we both need to cool off. I'll talk to him when I get back tomorrow afternoon. That way he'll know for sure I'm staying here."

At least she prayed he would understand. Once this final checkup from the specialist was done, she could cut the last tie to her past life, and turn all her attention toward the future.

Please, Lord, let that future include Noah and Chloe.

Chapter Twelve

Noah gripped the steering wheel with more force than necessary. New York. Beth was returning to New York. All her talk about staying in Dover was just that. Talk. Apparently her friend Kurt had convinced her that coming to work with him was too good an opportunity to pass up.

What hurt even more was how she'd accused him of deliberately sabotaging her building inspection. How could she think he'd be so underhanded? And if she was so upset that he'd nixed her building, why was she going back to New York?

He glanced out the window at the open country along the highway. Maybe he should have taken time to ask her. But the scalding shaft of pain in his chest had released all the old hurt from her walking away long ago. Instead, the anger had churned inside him all night, robbing him of sleep and darkening his mood all day. This was his last stop. Maybe then he could deal with Beth's defection and try to move forward.

The green-and-white sign for Old Agler Road flashed by, signaling he was nearing the old Victorian house. He was in no mood to deal with Harvey Kramer today. The man had no concern for his own safety or that of his crew, and balked at every regulation he had to adhere to. If Kramer had his way, he'd ignore building codes altogether.

If he hadn't promised Kramer he'd be here to check out the foundation problem, he'd turn around and have it out with Beth. Even if that meant going to New York to confront her. She'd left him so confused, he wasn't sure which way was up. All he knew for certain was that he didn't like being at odds with her. He didn't want to lose the connection that was reforming between them. The kiss they'd shared still had the power to warm his blood and send his heart pounding.

Flipping the turn signal lever, he eased the truck into the long, narrow driveway leading to the old home. It wouldn't take long to get under the house and identify the problems, but convincing his client to make the necessary reconstruction might take a while.

Kramer met him at the front door. "I hope you can come up with a quick and cheap solution to this floor issue. I'm losing time on this deal."

Noah followed him into the large kitchen on the northeast side of the house, noticing Kramer had ripped out cabinets and appliances in his haste to remodel. The man's impatience was also evident in the pulled-up floorboards, which now exposed the joists below. He also noticed the sagging ceiling had been braced. Unfortunately he'd done so with a few two-by-fours, which were far too weak to do the job safely. Noah pointed to the already bowing lumber. "You need to use two-by-sixes to hold that up."

Kramer waved him off. "I'll get around to it. It's all I had. So what about this floor?"

Noah flicked on his flashlight and examined the exposed wood beneath the floor, then began taking a few measurements. "I don't like what I'm seeing, but I'll have to get under the house to know for sure."

"Fine. Do it. I need to get the project on track before I lose my shirt."

Noah shook his head and went back to the truck, pulling out his blue coveralls and the tools he'd need to do a thorough foundation inspection.

A quick glance at the sky told him a rainstorm was on its way. He'd better get started. But between his truck and the opening to the crawl space, his thoughts reverted to Beth. He didn't want her to leave Dover. But how did he get her to stay? She'd gone to New York—but was it for good, or a quick trip to work out the details of a new job? He should have at least asked her before storming off. He'd considered calling her, but each time he'd lost his nerve. How could he convince her she needed to stay here with him and Chloe? Could they even compete with the life she'd once had?

Zipping up the coveralls, he flipped up the hood and got down on his knees. Thankfully the crawl space was reasonably spacious and allowed him plenty of headroom. He belly-crawled toward the corner, examining joists and foundation pilings as he went, not pleased with what he was seeing. When he reached the opening Kramer had made, he pulled out his tape measure and the flashlight again. Thunder rolled through the sky.

The floors definitely needed more joists to bring it up to code. The current ones were too small, and a couple were completely rotten. Rolling over, he scooted to the next pier block, which had sunk down nearly three inches into the poor soil. He took a couple pictures and made a few more measurements before preparing to crawl back out. As he maneuvered past another pier, he noticed a joist riddled with termite damage. How had he missed that? Simple answer—because he'd been constantly distracted by thoughts of Beth. He'd had to take each measurement twice because he couldn't keep the numbers in his head.

A closer look at the wood revealed the entire section was paper-thin. It could collapse at any moment. Time to get out of there. He stashed his tools in his belt and started forward on his stomach.

A loud snap sounded from overhead. Thunder? He reached forward, his feet digging into the soft dirt below the house. A loud crash. The house shook. A crack. Sudden weight pressed on his back, robbing him of air. Pain sliced into his thigh.

There was another rumble, then a blow to his head… then darkness.

Beth ducked in to the entryway, escaping the pouring rain, then stepped into the real estate office, unable to keep the smile from her face. Her mother glanced up. "Welcome home, sweetheart. How did it go?"

She placed her small suitcase and purse in the corner then sat down. "The doctor said I'm healing better than expected, and he even thinks I'll be able to do a little pointe work in time. Nothing long-term, but I might be able to dance a little."

"That's wonderful news. You must be excited."

"I am, but that's not the only thing that happened.

On the plane back, I sat with Katie Lorman. Remember her? We studied ballet together."

"I do. How is she?"

"Fine. She's working and dancing with Ballet Magnificat in Jackson, and she's asked me to join the staff working with the trainees. It's part-time, so I can still have my school and work with the ballet, too. Maybe even perform with them at some point." She didn't mention the one part of her plan that was still unsettled. Noah's place in her life.

Her mom held up her finger. "Speaking of your school, I did a little more digging on that blue building you liked." She tapped the keyboard then angled the computer so she could see. "It's on south Church Street, and it's in great shape. I looked it over this morning. Wood floors, lots of windows. It was an office complex, but it could easily be reconfigured to suit your needs."

Beth scrolled through the photos of the interior, her excitement growing. "It's adorable."

"I've already been in touch with the owner, and he's very motivated. And you won't need to worry about an inspection. He's already had that done, and I have the paperwork. In fact, I've started the purchase papers, too, and talked to Todd at the bank. All you have to do is take a look at the property, and we can get moving on it."

"You sound more excited about my new business than I am."

"I guess I am in a way. I like having you back home."

Beth wrapped her mother in a tight hug. "Thank you. I'm glad to be home, too." The reality of her decision landed on her mind, triggering a rush of insecurity.

"Mom, I've never started a business before. There's so much to think about, so much I don't know."

"Don't worry. I know exactly what to do. I'll walk you through every step. We'll come up with a business plan and get everything lined up."

The phone rang, and her mother answered. Beth looked at the photos again, mentally assigning each space to a part of her dance studio.

"Evelyn, what's wrong? Yes. She's here. She just got back."

Beth's heart seized when she saw the look of horror on her mother's face. "Yes. I will." She scribbled something on the notepad. "I'll notify the prayer chain."

Fear gripped her lungs. "Mom? What is it? Chloe?"

"No. Evelyn has been trying to reach you for the last half hour. Is your phone dead?"

She nodded. "I forgot my charger at the hotel."

Her mother took her hand. "It's Noah. He was doing a foundation inspection, and there was an accident."

Blood iced in her veins. "Is he—" She couldn't bring herself to ask the question.

"The house collapsed, and he's trapped underneath. The rescue squad is trying to get him out now, but it's a slow process. They don't want to cause another collapse."

"I've got to go. Where is he?" She took the paper from her mother. She recognized the road. The house belonged to Noah's first client, the difficult one.

"Maybe I should take you."

"No. I'm fine. I've got to go."

Her heart pounded so hard as she drove out of town she feared she couldn't breathe. Sweaty palms made gripping the steering wheel difficult. Fear like crashing waves ebbed and flowed in her stomach. A thousand questions darted through her mind. What if she lost him? Where was Chloe? How much of the house had collapsed? Why wasn't he more careful?

The answers didn't matter. She had to be there with him. He needed her. She needed him.

The pouring rain caused her to miss the driveway, and she lost precious time turning around. Fire and rescue trucks were parked next to the old Victorian, which was still standing. In her mind she'd imagined a pile of rubble. She grabbed her raincoat from the back and slipped it on as she hurried toward the activity, her feet sloshing on wet earth. She wanted to call his name, but he'd never hear her above the rain and thunder and the shouting of the workers. She looked around for a familiar face.

"Beth." Evelyn hurried toward her, wrapping her in a tight hug. "I'm so glad you're here."

"Where is he? Is he all right?"

Evelyn kept an arm around her waist as she walked her toward the back of the house. That's when she saw the corner of the house sagging awkwardly and a heap of rubble on the ground. "Oh, no. Is he under there?" Her heart beat in an unnatural rhythm, as if one chamber had shut down.

"Yes. They're working to get him out. All I know right now is that he's alive."

Beth glanced around at the men coming and going, walking slowly as if there was no urgency. "Why aren't they working harder? They have to get him out of there."

Evelyn patted her arm. "They're working as fast as

they can. They don't want to trigger another collapse, and the rain is making things difficult."

Beth's barely controlled emotions gave way. Tears poured down her cheeks, and a sob burst from her throat. "He has to be all right. I can't lose him now. I love him. Please, Lord, not now." She found herself in Evelyn's strong embrace as she cried, holding on to the woman tightly.

"Let's go sit in my car and get out of the rain. We can see everything from there. The chief promised he'd keep me updated."

Beth resisted moving. She needed to be right here when he came out. She wanted him to know she was here. "No, I'd better wait."

Evelyn pulled her around and urged her toward her vehicle parked a few yards away. Inside the warm, dry car, Beth was able to take a steady breath and think a little more clearly. "Where's Chloe? Does she know?"

Evelyn shook her head. "She's with friends. They were going to the movies in Sawyer's Bend. I'm not going to call her until we know something for certain."

After a half hour, Beth couldn't sit another moment. She got out and moved as close to the activity as she could. It was silly, but standing here in the rain, near Noah, made her feel like she was doing something. Lending moral support by her presence.

The next half hour saw progress. The firemen had shored up the area and were now under the house tending to Noah's injuries, but there was still a lot to do before they could safely remove him from the small space. He was unconscious.

Cold and wet, she returned to the car to wait with Noah's grandmother.

Evelyn took her hand, rubbing it to restore warmth to her skin. "You're freezing."

"I didn't notice." She laid her head back, closing her eyes. "He has to be all right. He has to be."

"That's what I'm praying for."

Beth squeezed Evelyn's hand. "I'm sorry. I should be trying to comfort you. I know you're as worried as I am."

"We both love him, don't we?"

"I always have. Life just got in our way."

"It happens." They sat in silence for another forty-five minutes, then Fire Chief O'Brian tapped on the car window.

"We're bringing him out now. He's still unconscious, but he's stable. He has a leg injury, and probably some cracked ribs. We're taking him to Magnolia County Hospital in Sawyer's Bend. You can meet us there."

"Can I see him?"

"He won't know you're here, but I guess it won't hurt."

Beth squeezed Evelyn's hand before getting out and hurrying toward the house. The rain had eased up. She stopped when she saw the men carrying the stretcher. She got as close as they would permit. Her heart was a cold lump in her chest. Noah had a wide brace around his neck, and his right leg was wrapped in thick covering. She ached to touch him to prove to herself he was alive, but she wasn't allowed that close. She had to settle for whispering his name and telling him she loved him.

She waited until the ambulance started off before getting into her car. Evelyn had left, probably to go get Chloe. Her impulse was to start the car and race to the hospital. But common sense prevailed. She took a moment to calm herself, then called her mother before she headed out.

By the time she arrived at the hospital, Noah was in surgery to repair damage to his leg, and all she could do was wait for Evelyn. Since she wasn't a relative and no one would tell her anything about his condition, she sought out the chapel. Her mind was so clouded by fear that she couldn't form a coherent prayer so she sat silently, knowing the Lord would understand her pleas.

She knew now that loving Noah and Chloe was more fulfilling than any starring role. She wanted to spend the rest of her life with them. She'd prove to him somehow that she'd never leave again. She'd stay by his side until he regained consciousness. She wanted to be the first person he saw when he woke up. Maybe then he'd understand that he was her obsession.

Noah fought his way through the gray fog of pain and confusion. He hurt, but he couldn't pinpoint where exactly. Thinking made his head throb. Something heavy was sitting on his chest, making it hard to breathe. He tried to move, only to regret it when pain shot through the right side of his body.

He heard his name being called. A soft feminine voice. Beth? He struggled to clear his thoughts, but the gray fog swirled around him again, drawing him down into darkness.

When he opened his eyes again, his vision was blurred. He blinked and glanced around, trying to grasp where he was. A hospital. He recoiled as the memory rushed back. The house. It had collapsed on top of him. He'd been too preoccupied with thoughts of Beth to notice the danger.

Beth. Was she here? He started to raise his head, only to wince and drop back down on the pillow.

"Noah. Oh, praise the Lord."

Gram? He closed his eyes to ease the ache and drifted off again.

"Daddy? Please wake up."

His vision was clear when he opened his eyes the next time, and he could process thoughts easier. "Chloe?"

Her little face held a bright smile. She leaned over the side rail and grasped his arm. "Daddy. You're awake."

He squeezed her hand, but his gaze searched the room. "Beth?"

"She's not here. She's talking to someone about a new job. I'll go get Gram."

Before he could speak, Chloe darted away, leaving him with a new ache that twisted deeper into his core than any physical pain. She'd left. The job had won. His gut kicked, stirring up the old sediment of resentment. When would he learn?

"Noah. Oh, my dear boy, it's so good to have you back. You had us worried."

He tried to force a smile for her sake but failed.

"How do you feel?"

"I'll survive." He'd survive his injuries. But not Beth's defection. "Has she left?"

"Who?"

"Beth?"

"No. She's right here. She's on the phone. I'll go get her. She'll want to talk to you."

"Don't bother. I know what she'll say."

"You're not making sense. Maybe I should call the nurse." She reached for the call button.

"Chloe told me Beth was taking a new job. I know all about it. There's nothing I need to say to her. I knew she'd never stay in Dover. Once that friend offered her a job, I knew she'd jump at the chance. I can't depend on her to hang around."

He glanced up as someone stepped close to the foot of the bed. Beth. His heart swelled with affection. She was the only thing he wanted to see when he woke up, and his muddled brain had dangled her image in his mind repeatedly. But she'd been smiling, and she wasn't now.

"You'll never change, will you? I could start a dozen dance schools here in Dover, and you'd still be waiting for me to walk away."

"Dance studio?" What was she talking about?

"If I miss your call, or if I leave town for some reason, your first thought will always be that I've left again. Well, I'm done, Noah. I won't live like that."

Tears were seeping from her eyes. "I'm glad you're going to be all right."

He reached out to her, but she spun and walked out. "Beth."

Gram pressed him back against the pillow, her stern expression clearly revealing her distress. "Honestly, you are the most blind, closed-minded man I ever knew. Worse than your granddad and your father. I'll have you know that young woman has been here at your side from the beginning. She stood in the pouring rain while they dug you out from under that house. She's been here at your bedside around-the-clock the last two days, refusing to even eat. Her mother brought her food because she was afraid you'd wake up while she was down in the cafeteria. Francie had to bring her fresh clothes."

"Gram."

"I'm not finished. Beth loves you, and if you don't come to your senses, you're going to lose her again. You listen to me. I know you're protecting your heart from being broken again. But that's not your job. You're not strong enough to do that alone. You're supposed to give your heart, all of it, to the Lord so He can heal it and return it to you able to love again."

Noah knew she was right. It was the one thing he'd never been able to turn over to God because he feared he'd be opening himself to disappointment and failure again.

He loved Beth. He'd made a mistake and jumped to conclusions because she hadn't been the first thing he'd seen when he'd awakened. Now he had to fix the mess he'd made. "Gram, call her, tell her I didn't understand. She'll listen to you."

"Not on your life." Gram shoved her hand into her purse and pulled out her phone, laying it firmly on his chest. "Do your own dirty work."

Chloe had come to the side of the bed and frowned at him. "Daddy, Miss Beth isn't like Mom. She loves me."

Gram took Chloe's hand. "Even your daughter sees more clearly than you do. We'll be back later. The doctors say you can go home tomorrow, and I have to get the house ready. Come along, Chloe. Let's leave your father to stew in his own sour juices awhile."

"What does that mean?"

"I'll explain on the way home."

Noah stared at the cell phone a long while before finding the courage to call Beth. It went straight to voice mail. Four more tries brought the same result. He left messages, but he was beginning to fear Beth would never listen to them.

It hit him then that she might leave Dover after this. And it would be entirely his fault this time.

Beth strolled through the lower rooms of her new dance studio. Things had moved quickly, and she'd signed the papers first thing this morning. Her mother had handled all the details and greased some wheels along the way. Beth had wanted to be involved with every aspect of her new venture, but she'd been too concerned about Noah to leave the hospital.

That was proving to be a pointless endeavor. She'd stayed by his side every moment, but all he could see when he woke was that she wasn't there. His first reaction had been to assume she'd left again. She'd done all she could to convince him. Now it was time to let go and move on.

Turning her attention to the building again, she stepped into a small room at the back that held a sink and small fridge. She could expand this to accommodate a full kitchen. She would be spending many hours here now. Retracing her steps, she went back to the front of the store. The room on the left would be her office, and with a little remodeling she could have two large rooms downstairs and two upstairs. It was all working out perfectly. All that remained was to complete the business paperwork and decide on a name for her new dance school. She was undecided between

Bethany's School of Dance and Montgomery's Dance Academy.

Hopefully the countless details of setting up her school would keep her mind off Noah. The thought of him never failed to send a spike of pain into her chest and moisture to her eyes. He'd called repeatedly, and left messages begging her to talk to him. As much as she longed to, she knew it was futile. She had to find a way to let go before she went nuts.

The bell sound on her cell phone was a welcome interruption—until she saw the name on the text message. Evelyn. Her heart ballooned into her throat as she read the words. Noah needs you. How soon can you get here?

Please, Lord, let him be all right. What had happened? Had he relapsed? Fallen? The drive to Noah's was only a few blocks, but it felt like forever. She hurried to the front door and didn't bother to knock. "Evelyn." She went into the front parlor and stopped. Noah was coming toward her, moving slowly, his hand clutching a cane. He looked pale but better than he had in the hospital. The chambray button-up shirt he wore matched the blue of his eyes. Eyes that were bright with affection and curiosity.

"Beth. What are you doing here?"

She scanned his tall frame, searching for something wrong. The bandage was still on his temple where the board had struck him, but it was smaller today. Otherwise he looked fine. A bit pale but solid. Strong. "Evelyn said you needed me and to come right away."

Noah frowned then nodded slowly. "I see. She's right. I do need you."

Beth took a step backward. Obviously Evelyn was

trying to get them to work out their differences. But it was too late. "You look perfectly fine to me. I have to go." She whirled, but Noah called out to her.

"Please don't leave. I can't chase after you in my condition. Won't you take pity on a guy who has no sense, who let fear rule his life for so long it might have cost him the only woman he's ever loved?"

She closed her eyes, willing herself not to rush into his arms.

"Forgive me. Gram told me how you stayed with me through all this. I think I knew that on some level because the only images I remember during that time were of you. When I woke up and you weren't there I—"

She heard him take an unsteady breath. Were his ribs hurting him? She faced him, the love in his eyes making her breath catch.

"I wanted to crawl back into the dark and never come out."

He took a few slow steps toward her, never taking his eyes from hers. "Beth, please forgive me. I don't want to lose you again. I love you. Chloe loves you. We belong together."

"How can I trust that you won't always think I'll leave?"

"Because I heard about your dance school and your position with Ballet Magnificat. But mostly because I'm going to love you so much you'll never want to go anywhere else but in my arms. Beth, you're my family. You're where I fit."

Her tears blurred his handsome face. She swiped them away and met him in the middle of the room. "And I fit with you."

He wrapped her in his arms, letting the cane fall to the floor with a thud. She held him close, too close. He grunted. She'd forgotten about his ribs.

"I'm sorry."

He shook his head. "No. It's worth the pain to hold you close." He kissed her tenderly, cradling her face in his palms. "Marry me."

"Yes. Oh, yes." She kissed him before sliding her arms around him and snuggling close to his chest. She wanted to stay here forever. "When?"

He chuckled. "Are you in a hurry?"

"Oh, yes. We've waited too long to find each other again."

He stepped back and pointed to the cane on the floor. "Let's sit and talk about it."

After handing him the cane, she slipped an arm around his waist to steady him, and to feel his warm presence. She sat on the arm of the chair, her hand holding his, unwilling to let go.

"I thought you'd want a big wedding with all the trimmings."

"No. Not big. Fast."

He laughed and squeezed her hand. "Lady, you make a man feel like a king. All right, when do you suggest?"

She took a moment to orient her dates. "Christmas Eve?"

"That's only three days away. Are you sure?"

"What about Christmas Eve eve, would that be better?"

Noah pulled her down and kissed her again. "Today would be perfect, but I think there are a few legalities to take care of." He captured her mouth again, kissing her with all the love and promise she knew he held in his heart.

"Gram. I think they made up."

Chloe's voice drew them apart. Beth stood, taking a place behind him, her hands resting on his broad shoulders.

"Are you getting married now?" Chloe's tone was filled with hopeful excitement.

"Yes. We are."

"Oh, Daddy." She threw her arms around his neck and squeezed. "You've given me the best present ever. A mom for Christmas."

"What's this I hear about wedding bells?" Gram joined them, her smile wide and loving. "I knew if I could just get you two knuckleheads in the same room, it would all work out. So when is the wedding?"

Beth bit her lower lip. "Christmas Eve."

"Oh, my. Then I need to get busy. It'll be too late to get the church. We'll have the ceremony here. Thank goodness I had the house professionally decorated for the holidays. I'll call Francie about food. But you'd better talk to her first. I know she'll be thrilled at the news."

"Wow. A wedding right here. That's so cool." Chloe gave Beth a hug. "Miss Beth, is it okay if I call you Mom?"

She glanced at Noah before answering. "Yes, but do you think your mother will be okay with that?"

"She won't care. She always wanted me to call her Yvonne anyway."

Gram gathered Chloe away to start making preparations, leaving them alone again.

Noah rose to his feet again and tugged her into his arms. "There's just one more thing I need from you."

"Anything."

He touched his wounded leg. "You helped Chloe and Gram. Do you think you could teach me to dance—to help with my leg, of course?"

She laughed and caressed his face with her palm. "I would love to teach you to dance. In fact, I have the perfect studio. All it needs is a name."

Noah kissed her lips, letting his finger trace a path across her lower lip and up her chin. "I was thinking Carlisle's School of Dance sounds nice."

"I think it sounds perfect."

* * * * *

*If you loved this tale of sweet romance,
pick up these other stories
in the* HOME TO DOVER *series
from author Lorraine Beatty.*

*REKINDLED ROMANCE
RESTORING HIS HEART
PROTECTING THE WIDOW'S HEART
HIS SMALL-TOWN FAMILY
BACHELOR TO THE RESCUE
HER CHRISTMAS HERO
THE NANNY'S SECRET CHILD*

Available now from Love Inspired!

Find more great reads at www.LoveInspired.com.

Dear Reader,

Thank you for visiting Dover again. I hope you enjoyed meeting the next Montgomery sibling, Bethany. Like most of us, Beth struggled to find a balance in her life between her career, her family and her faith. In her ambition to rise to the top of her profession, she ignored important parts of her life. In losing the thing she loved most, her ability to dance, Beth was forced to reexamine her life and her priorities.

We're told to put God first, but life has a way of overshadowing that commandment. It's especially difficult for those of us in the arts. Whether we are dancers, artists, writers, musicians or actors, we hone our skills, which are fueled by love of our art and our determination to excel, but with little or no monetary compensation. Many times we ask the Lord if this is what we're supposed to be doing because the journey seems so pointless.

With the help of Noah and Chloe, the Lord shows Beth that He has unlimited blessings to lavish on his children, and if we keep our hearts and minds open, we can find new dreams.

I love to hear from readers. You can reach me through my website: lorrainebeatty.com. From there, you can access my Facebook page and other social media links. Or, you can write to Love Inspired, 195 Broadway, New York, NY 10007.

Lorraine Beatty

REQUEST YOUR FREE BOOKS!

2 FREE INSPIRATIONAL NOVELS
PLUS 2
FREE
MYSTERY GIFTS

Love Inspired®

YES! Please send me 2 FREE Love Inspired® novels and my 2 FREE mystery gifts (gifts are worth about $10). After receiving them, if I don't wish to receive any more books, I can return the shipping statement marked "cancel." If I don't cancel, I will receive 6 brand-new novels every month and be billed just $4.99 per book in the U.S. or $5.49 per book in Canada. That's a saving of at least 17% off the cover price. It's quite a bargain! Shipping and handling is just 50¢ per book in the U.S. and 75¢ per book in Canada.* I understand that accepting the 2 free books and gifts places me under no obligation to buy anything. I can always return a shipment and cancel at any time. Even if I never buy another book, the two free books and gifts are mine to keep forever.   105/305 IDN GH5P

Name _____ (PLEASE PRINT) _____

Address _____ Apt. #

City _____ State/Prov. _____ Zip/Postal Code

Signature (if under 18, a parent or guardian must sign)

Mail to the **Reader Service:**
IN U.S.A.: P.O. Box 1867, Buffalo, NY 14240-1867
IN CANADA: P.O. Box 609, Fort Erie, Ontario L2A 5X3

Are you a subscriber to Love Inspired® books
and want to receive the larger-print edition?
Call 1-800-873-8635 or visit www.ReaderService.com.

---

* Terms and prices subject to change without notice. Prices do not include applicable taxes. Sales tax applicable in N.Y. Canadian residents will be charged applicable taxes. Offer not valid in Quebec. This offer is limited to one order per household. Not valid for current subscribers to Love Inspired books. All orders subject to credit approval. Credit or debit balances in a customer's account(s) may be offset by any other outstanding balance owed by or to the customer. Please allow 4 to 6 weeks for delivery. Offer available while quantities last.

Your Privacy—The Reader Service is committed to protecting your privacy. Our Privacy Policy is available online at www.ReaderService.com or upon request from the Reader Service.

We make a portion of our mailing list available to reputable third parties that offer products we believe may interest you. If you prefer that we not exchange your name with third parties, or if you wish to clarify or modify your communication preferences, please visit us at www.ReaderService.com/consumerchoice or write to us at Reader Service Preference Service, P.O. Box 9062, Buffalo, NY 14240-9062. Include your complete name and address.

LII5

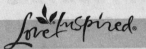
*Could a Christmastime nanny position for the ranch
foreman's son turn into a full-time new family for one
Texas teacher?*

*Read on for a sneak preview of the third book in the
LONE STAR COWBOY LEAGUE: BOYS RANCH
miniseries, THE NANNY'S TEXAS CHRISTMAS*
by *Lee Tobin McClain*.

"Am I in trouble?" Logan asked, sniffling.

How did you discipline a kid when his whole life had
just flashed before your eyes? Flint schooled his features
into firmness. "One thing's for sure, tractors are going to
be off-limits for a long time."

Logan just buried his head in Flint's shoulder.

As they all started walking again, Flint felt that delicate
hand on his arm once more.

"You doing okay?" Lana Alvarez asked.

He shook his head. "I just got a few more gray hairs. I
should've been watching him better."

"Maybe so," Marnie said. "But you can't, not with all
the work you have at the ranch. So I think we can all
agree—you need a babysitter for Logan." She stepped in
front of Lana and Flint, causing them both to stop. "And
the right person to do it is here. Miss Lana Alvarez."

"Oh, Flint doesn't want—"

"You've got time after school. And a Christmas
vacation coming up." Marnie crossed her arms, looking

determined. "Logan already loves you. You could help to keep him safe and happy."

Flint's desire to keep Lana at a distance tried to raise its head, but his worry about his son, his gratitude about Logan's safety, and the sheer terror he'd just been through, put his own concerns into perspective.

Logan took priority. And if Lana would agree to be Logan's nanny on a temporary basis, that would be best for Logan.

And Flint would tolerate her nearness. Somehow.

"Can she, Daddy?" Logan asked, his face eager.

He turned to Lana, who looked like she was facing a firing squad. "Can you?" he asked her.

"Please, Miss Alvarez?" Logan chimed in.

Lana drew in a breath and studied them both, and Flint could almost see the wheels turning in her brain.

He could see mixed feelings on her face, too. Fondness for Logan. Mistrust of Flint himself.

Maybe a little bit of… What was that hint of pain that wrinkled her forehead and darkened her eyes?

Flint felt like he was holding his breath.

Finally, Lana gave a definitive nod. "All right," she said. "We can try it. But I'm going to have some very definite rules for you, young man." She looked at Logan with mock sternness.

As they started walking toward the house again, Lana gave Flint a cool stare that made him think she might have some definite rules for him, too.

Don't miss
THE NANNY'S TEXAS CHRISTMAS
by Lee Tobin McClain, available December 2016
wherever Love Inspired® books and ebooks are sold.

www.LoveInspired.com

LIEXP1116